"Piercing . . . A great talent."

—Elena Tanakova, *Gallerix*

"This story is not about disaster, but about what happens to the survivors . . . This is the new Russian prose."

—Vladimir Pankratov

"*Stories of a Life* is a kaleidoscopic ode to the power of storytelling. Nataliya Meshchaninova's voice is fearless and resonant. She writes with striking openness, humor, and a ferocious heart."

—Gina Nutt, author of *Night Rooms*

"Strikes with unexpected force."

—Elena Makeenko, *Gorky Media*

"It is not often that people are ready to open up, and only the willingness to open up distinguishes real literature."

—Aglaya Kurnosenko

Stories of a Life

Nataliya Meshchaninova

translated from the Russian by
Fiona Bell

DEEP VELLUM PUBLISHING
DALLAS, TEXAS

Deep Vellum Publishing
3000 Commerce St., Dallas, Texas 75226
deepvellum.org · @deepvellum

Deep Vellum is a 501c3 nonprofit literary arts organization
founded in 2013 with the mission to bring
the world into conversation through literature.

Support for this publication has been provided in part by the
Mikhail Prokhorov Fund's Transcript Program.

ISBNs:
978-1-64605-115-1 (paperback)
978-1-64605-116-8 (ebook)

LIBRARY OF CONGRESS CONTROL NUMBER: 2021946897

Front cover design by Natalya Balnova

Interior Layout and Typesetting by KGT

Printed in the United States of America

CONTENTS

A Little Bit about My Family

MY MOM WRITES PATRIOTIC SONGS ABOUT Russia and sings them in churches. She tours around coastal towns, performing. She sees a solo album on the horizon.

Her husband (my fourth stepfather) is building a house out of straw.

My older sister lives in Germany. She is a Jehovah's Witness preparing for Armageddon. After that, she will live happily with tigers and other animals, sitting around a campfire singing "Kumbaya" (there won't be any predators after Armageddon).

My younger sister is the assistant to the deputy. She kisses the governor on both cheeks every May Day.

My brother is very fat and married to a woman twenty years older than him. She smacks him around a little, but he tolerates and loves her.

My nephew is in prison for stealing a car. It's his third time there. Always for grand theft auto. And he never plans on selling the cars, he just likes taking joyrides. Pure bliss, until the first traffic police checkpoint, and then two or three years in prison. The cycle continues.

My aunt has hanged herself a few times. Not very successfully. That's why she became an alcoholic.

I decided, for some reason, that I'm a director.

There isn't a single normal person in our family. Sorry in advance.

Fears

EVER SINCE I WAS A KID, ALMOST ALL my fears have been about my mother. I don't know if this is because she had heart problems (born with a defect), or because until I was six, I only saw her hysterical, never happy . . . Anyway, by the time my milk teeth came in, my greatest fear was that she would die. A car would hit her. Yes, she'd be on her way home from work and get hit by a car. Maybe she'd already been hit. I'd look outside, sitting like a frog on the windowsill. She's not coming home from work. Here's the bus, everyone's getting off at the stop, trailing home like ants. But Mom's not there. She's definitely been hit by a car! Or maybe not. She'd fall out the window. She'd just be hanging the laundry or washing the window when she'd lose her balance. She would fall. Good luck surviving a fall from the fifth floor. Or maybe not. She would die of a heart attack. She'd already had one before. She wouldn't survive a second one. Or what if something happened to me? She'd die of grief. Or of a heart attack brought on by grief . . .

Never upset Mom—I learned that quickly. That's why I became an expert at lying before I was even out of diapers. My lies didn't stop her from worrying, but they did make me feel like I was guarding her, and my fear for her life receded a little. As far as my mom knew, I was always doing great. I got straight As, went to clubs, wrote poetry, and put the toys away in my room. My fear of upsetting my mother was stronger than the truth, stronger than my own self-interest. My fear of losing her was paralyzing.

I was also terrified of war. I don't know where this fear came from, since no one ever told me any scary stories. Even though Grandpa was wounded in the war, he never stirred my imagination with his memories of battle. I didn't watch war movies, either—even the thought was unbearable. I think my fear of war came from my dreams. I had them often, almost always the same way. I was a man, a soldier, rushing across a field toward the forest. There was a German helicopter flying above me, and I felt the machine-gun fire plowing across the wet grass and finally overtaking me. Always like that: I got stitched through with a line of huge bullets and it hurt like hell. I heard triumphant German voices. Then I died. Afterward I woke up, but I couldn't move my arms or legs, and I couldn't scream either, so I lay there dead as a doornail and thought, *Now that I've been killed at war, Mom will definitely die of grief.* These war dreams crawled over me night after night, rustling like cockroaches. They alternated with dreams where my mom fell off a cliff and hit the rocks below with a thud.

My friend told me to write my fear down on a piece of paper, as if it had already happened. Most important, it had to be in secret code. Then my fear would go away. I'd learned a code somewhere: first you write the alphabet from top to bottom, then on the other side you write it bottom to top. You end up with A-Z, B-Y, C-X, and so on. I wrote the following in code: "Nln tlg srg yb z xzi" ("Mom got hit by a car"). I put the note somewhere on my shelf. My mom found it and thought that I'd been sleep-walking again. She took it to show the women at work what nonsense I had written in my sleep. The women were alarmed but eventually forgot about it. A few years later, Mom actually did get hit by a car and barely survived. Everyone who knew her donated liters of blood. I begged the hospital to take more blood, more! Every week I went to the donation center and they chased me out because you're not allowed to give blood that often. For a long time, my mom was on the edge of death and I lived in her hospital ward. When she was sleeping very quietly, I watched her stomach nervously. Phew, all right, it's still moving, just barely visible. She's breathing, she's alive. I blamed myself for everything. Why did I write that note, and in code, no less? I thought it worked like a spell: whatever you wrote came true. This theory was confirmed a few more times, but overall it wasn't exactly scientifically proven, so no one believed me when I said, "Never write bad things—they'll come true."

All that came later, though. Back then, when I was a kid, my fear of my mom's death was unsubstantiated. But that loss already existed somewhere inside me, and whenever I thought about it, I felt a viscid pain. I never told my mom.

But I had more important things to worry about! The troublemakers. Scary, disgusting groups of pimply teenagers in front of the school. Their dirty hands, stinking of tobacco, tugging at your skirt, which was two years old but still pretty clean. On my way to school I waited until I spotted a teacher to cling on to. "Heyyyyyyy, Inna Aleksandrovna! I'll walk with you! Yep! Great! Of course, I did my homework!"

The whole class was nothing but troublemakers. One girl was always masturbating in literature class, her face all red. Everyone except the teacher knew what she was doing. After class, in the back room—oh, the things they did to her. She was too ashamed to scream, but she did huff and puff. It was scary, so scary. Between periods, you had to rush out into the hallway—even if it meant taking a smack on the butt and a blow to the ego—just so you didn't hear the noise coming from the back room, that girl, that stifled laughter, that strange yelping. Why didn't the teachers notice anything? Why did they sleepwalk to the teachers' lounge as soon as the bell rang? Why did they allow that huffing and puffing in the back room?

Mom, I'm not going to school today. Mom, my foot. My foot hurts a lot. I don't need to go to the doctor, it's rheumatism. (How did I come up with that?) My mom believed me, somehow. She believed every lie I told, no matter how ridiculous.

It's evening. My mom yells from the hallway: "Natasha! Someone's here for you!" In the doorway behind her I see HIM, the worst of the worst. I pass his apartment every day; he lives on the second floor. As I run past his door, I always feel like he's watching me through the peephole and sneering with the most wretched, depraved smirk.

MOTH-ER! Why can't you see— he's one of the troublemakers! Mom! Why are you calling me to the door? Why didn't you tell him I'm not here? I'm not home and never will be. Why aren't you grabbing him by the ear and threatening to hurt him? How come you're calling me with that sing-song voice, as if my best friend is over to fold origami???

I went out to see him. His eyes grazed over me, and for some reason he kicked between my legs. Right under the balls, if I'd had any. "Tomorrow you're gonna bring me money. As much as you got. Or else I'll jump on you from a tree."

He started jumping on me from trees regularly, since I didn't have any money to my name. They must have taught the troublemakers how to jump from trees or something . . .

I gathered my things and some food and started off along the railroad tracks. To Moscow. I'd heard it was best to travel north. But since I'd blabbed to one of my friends about running away,

I was brought back before evening. My mom was wringing her hands. I realized I hadn't protected her peace of mind, that my dreams of Moscow had been an unacceptable luxury. I had to find a way to survive here.

I had to become one of the trouble-makers. There were no good kids in my town, nowhere for them to come from. All the kids were troublemakers: bad, disgusting, and extremely dangerous. They played dangerous games in the woods by the railroad tracks. Oh, the things that went on in those woods, which were filled with flowering acacias and the trills of nightingales.

At age five, they tied girls to trees and whipped them with stinging nettles until they went into hysterics and their entire bodies turned red. Then you had to lie to your mom, saying you acciden-tally fell into some nettles.

At age ten, they made you lie on the ties between the rails and wait for an incoming train to pass over you, and you weren't allowed to crap your pants. They forced all the kids to lie down there, but one boy stayed the whole time. Afterward, his mom took him to live in the city with his grandma for good. We never saw him again. Obviously, the boy had crapped his pants and was also a bad liar. He deserved our contempt, and we never mentioned him again.

I felt ashamed and tried not to think about him, but the boy who crapped his pants haunted me. I wished he'd send me a letter. I wished he'd write something like, "I didn't crap my pants. I'm living with my grandma because she's near death and needs care. After I lay beneath the train, everything became clear and I became a man. Tell everyone I say hello . . .

and so on. But, of course, he didn't send a letter. They took him to his grandma's so he'd be far away from us troublemakers. I didn't have that kind of grandma. I had one, but I couldn't go live with her because she thought I stuffed my face, and she had little patience for grandchildren anyway.

In general, seeking protection from adults was a lost cause. You couldn't trust them, either. I really burned my fingers learning that lesson. One day I skipped my after-school program and wandered through town, trying to kill time. My mom was at work and I didn't have the key to the apartment. I had a snack at my neighbor's. I was hanging out in front of a store when this guy rode up to me on a bicycle. I'd never seen him before. He was good-looking. He told me he was a friend of my dad's. My dad had been living with another family for a few years now, so I had no clue who his friends were. I had no reason to doubt that he was friends with this nice man on a bicycle. We went for a ride. He took me around town for a bit, then said, "Let's go to the woods."

It was warm, April or May, and the woods were already green and fragrant. We entered the woods like in a fairy tale. The grass was tall and dense. Dad's friend helped me off the bike, then followed. "Do you want to lie down?" he suggested as he reclined on the grass. I lay down, too. He said, "You know, it feels good to lie in the grass naked." I wasn't sure about this, since I'd done it before, and afterward my whole body itched for three days. But Dad's friend was pretty self-assured and started taking off his pants.

Luckily, Dad's friend had never been to our woods and didn't know that people often walked through them on their way from the train. The woods were covered with footpaths, but Dad's friend didn't notice them in the tall grass. When he took off his pants, people passed by, having popped up quietly on the paths. Dad's friend was spooked. But then something terrible happened: a teacher from my after-school program came down the path. She saw me lying there with Dad's friend, who was buckling his belt and smiling nervously. "Well, well, well . . ." she said. As she uttered this, I pressed myself into the ground. Dad's friend did, too. Then she said, "Well, now! Who are you, exactly?" He stuttered, saying that he was a friend of my father's. She said, "And what is her father's name, I wonder?" He replied, "Nikolai . . . Petrovich?" "No!" she said triumphantly, "His name is Viktor Fyodorovich." I stared at Dad's friend with contempt and shook my head. *Shame on you,* I thought. *Shame! And we could have been such good friends!*

They took a while to straighten things out. She wanted to call the police, but there weren't cell phones back then, you had to go find a pay phone. Dad's fake friend refused to go anywhere. They bickered for five minutes, and then he disappeared.

The teacher turned her attention to me. She walked me home, yelling the whole way, and when she found my mom at the store, she started yelling at her even more loudly, telling her in the gravest tone about how I'd been fooling around with Dad's friend.

Traitor, I thought. *Vile creature. She doesn't get it. She doesn't have a brain! She doesn't understand you're not supposed to upset my mom, she won't survive a second heart attack!*

My mom took me home and, out of helplessness, beat the shit out of me with a jump rope. At that point, I understood very clearly that having grown-up friends wasn't an option.

I wanted to be friends with ghosts, or imaginary people, or aliens. I wanted them to be strong and honest, to protect me. Everyone else was scared of ghosts, while I was trying to arrange meetings with them. It never worked out. Although a few times I pretended to make contact with a spirit in front of my mom, and she believed me. Then she told the women at work about how I was not only a sleepwalker, but also a medium. Reveling in my lies, I told my mom about people who'd come back from the dead, who'd landed from outer space. But I never met real dead people. Which sucks. My whole life, I've never met a single spirit. I've had only real friends, the kind made of flesh and blood.

By now our dangerous group had grown up a little. We got into cigarettes, weed, and alcohol, always in the woods. The teenage sex began.

And then a horrifying piece of news rocked the whole town, devastating even the worst people. "Seven teenagers brutally raped and killed a fifth-grader in the woods. They sewed his mouth shut so he wouldn't scream, stuck barbed wire into his anus and twisted it until it came out of his throat . . ." There were very detailed descriptions, horrible to imagine. The teenagers were caught and put in prison somewhere, but within two years every single one had been released, and they came to our nightclub at the cultural center. The seven murderers stood with beers in their hands and watched the dancing girls who, for some reason, started flailing even harder when they noticed the murderers' gazes. Back then, it was very fashionable to flail while dancing. An employee from the cultural association chaperoned us the entire night. Vera Fyodorovna, a forty-five-year-old woman. She watched serenely as the girls twisted and writhed and the murderers nursed their beers. She wore the light half-smile of someone who had everything under control: girls and murderers alike.

You had to leave the nightclub earlier than everyone else, pretending you weren't really leaving at all, just stepping out for some air and coming right back. But really, you'd crouch unnoticed along the parapets and the flowerbeds, in the shadows. Then you'd cross the road, walk under the trees, and go home, go home! You wouldn't want any

of the murderers to follow you. You'd
want them to think you're still flailing
beside them, and that later they might
have the chance to "walk you home"—
that is, chase you, catch you, and fuck
you in the woods. But most important,
you had to leave early so that you could
slip past that second-floor entryway
where the tree-jumper lurked unnoticed.
Then, quietly, trying to walk without
making a sound, you'd almost reach the
fifth floor. But you'd have to make sure
in advance that there wasn't anybody
on the last dark flight of stairs between
the fourth and fifth floors. Because there
often would be someone who turned out
the lights and waited for me, wouldn't
let me go home to my mom, who went
to bed early and slept blissfully unaware
that in her very entryway her daughter
was being groped by some shady types.
Future murderers for sure. Sleep, Mom,

sleep in your cradle of grapevines. He's got barbed wire in his pocket, he's about to take it out, tomorrow everyone will be horrified, and you, of course, will die of grief.

Later someone slashed the padding on our door. *C-c-c-cut*, like that, slashed the knife's entire length. He was so angry, he even wrote "Natasha, suck a dick" on the entryway wall. Yellow cotton batting bulged shamelessly from the wound. What a disgrace! Afterward someone painted over the graffiti. We stitched up the door. Then someone slashed it again, this time in a different area. We stitched it up again.

A new nightmare appeared in my repertoire. I'd go up to the fifth floor, where I saw the evil tree-jumper, his dick hanging out. He would cut open the door with a knife, and blood flowed from it. Because the door . . . the door was my mother. The whole landing was covered in blood, the knife and the tree-jumper's dick were covered in blood. The dream recurred with impressive regularity, eclipsing my war dreams. Those sweet, heroic war dreams . . .

"Mom, let's move! We could move to Abrau-Durso? To the settlements? To Bumblefuck, Nowhere!"

"Yeah, yeah, we'll move," my mom said vacantly. "We've always wanted to go to Kamchatka!"

"Mom, I'm serious! I can't live here!"

"OK, OK! We'll definitely move one day!"

"Now, Mom, now!"

To this day, she hasn't moved. She still lives among murderers and tree-jumpers who by now have married, procreated, and gotten fat. She lives in an apartment with a scarred, stitch-weary quilted door. On her way to the store she walks past murderers sitting outside with strollers, munching on sunflower seeds. They say hello to her. Things have calmed down. No one's lurking on the fifth floor.

I visited her and peeked into all the corners of my fear with a bottle of cognac in my hand and my husband on my arm. We drank a lot, wandered around the town drunk, and ridiculed these fears. I doubled over with laughter. I hoped my hooting would stifle the deathly chill in my stomach. The deathly chill of the German lead, the barbed wire, the steel knife blade, and that terrible, naked dick.

Literary Exhibitionism

WHEN I WAS FOURTEEN, I READ *The Secret Diary of Laura Palmer* and decided if I didn't start writing my own diary, then no one would ever know how I lived and died. (At fourteen I wanted to be killed in a tasteful, high-profile way.) I bought a notebook, wrote the date on the first page, and began like Laura Palmer: "Dear Diary . . ." After that, I wasn't sure what to do. I had to introduce myself somehow. I wrote something like:

*My name is Natasha, I'm 14
years old, and I'm in 9th grade.
I do sports: kayaking and
canoeing. And I have a huge
crush on Sasha Shipulin. He's
going to be a kayaking cham-
pion one day. But he doesn't
like me back. He's so cute and
I have zits. Mom said I should
bake him* pirozhki *because the
way to a man's heart is through
his stomach. I'm learning to
bake* pirozhki *made from yeast
dough in the oven.*

I reread my entry. I didn't like what I'd
written for two reasons. First of all, it
reminded me of a school essay, and that
wasn't what I was going for. Second,
from the very first page, I'd described
myself in this way . . . as if I were hid-
eous and fat. And I wasn't. I did have

zits, but my friend Marina said they went away as soon as you fucked a guy. She was already fucking and had verified this personally: her zits had disappeared. That's why I didn't want to immortalize my zits or those stupid *pirozhki*, because all that would change soon. And, besides, comparing my first few lines to Laura Palmer's diary, I realized all mine was good for was a laugh.

So I ripped that page out.

I didn't want to write about mundane life. Describing every single day, what I did, who said what to me, what happened—that was child's play. I wanted to write about my inner world. About what excited me.

The diary should start in a mysterious tone, I thought. On a new page I wrote something like: "I am Natalie. I'm 14 years old, but already mature enough..." I liked what I'd written, about how I was already mature enough. It wasn't clear what I was mature enough *for*, but it was good. A promising start. I continued: "My love overwhelms me" (no need to mention that it was unrequited). "My beloved is a handsome man with sensual lips. Yesterday, as I walked through the park on my way home from practice" (no need to say what sport, it lent some mystery), "my heart began pounding. I sensed that he was gaining on me, my demon, my dark angel . . . I turned around, the wind ruffled my blond hair, and I saw him approaching quickly! What came next, I won't describe here . . . but it was dizzying. For a long time after, my lips were sore and itchy and his scent lingered on my hands. He walked me to the bus and then retreated into the night. I await my meeting with him tomorrow, tomorrow by the Fantômas statue . . ."

I was pleased with my writing. Very pleased, indeed. It was like the beginning of one of those novels with detailed sex scenes. I'd read one when I was just twelve. It was called something like *The Whore of Venice*. Thanks to that book, I learned everything about Venice, mastered some Italian phrases, and stole a few metaphors for copulation. I didn't want to call sex "sex." Stuff like "the unicorn burst into the valley" seemed more literary and highbrow to me.

Now satisfied with the first page of my diary, I moved on. Although, of course, none of it bore any relation to reality. That evening, after practice ended, I paced outside the boys' locker room for a long time, waiting for Shipulin to leave. Eventually someone scared me off. I walked toward the park and decided to sit in the reeds by the water and watch the road. When I saw Shipulin a ways away, I was going to sneak out from the reeds and start walking in front of him slowly. He was faster than me, so he would catch up and we would start talking and then he would walk me to the bus. I'd used this trick a few times before, and it had worked. Once Shipulin not only walked me to the bus, but he even bought me a meat pie!

But that evening I climbed too far into the reeds (it was early spring, wet), and my sneakers slid into the smelly, sticky, green muck. I burst into tears and couldn't stop crying for a while. It wasn't just that it was wet and disgusting, it also smelled terrible! Then Shipulin appeared down the road not alone but with three boys from his team. I had to sit in the reeds because I couldn't let them see me in those sneakers. They passed without noticing me (it was already dark), and I trudged to the bus, still sobbing.

I was ashamed to write about that in my diary. Anyone who read it wouldn't want to keep reading and wouldn't find out what a gutsy, proud, mysterious, blonde beauty I was. By the way, I wasn't a blonde. I've had mousy hair since I was born. But! In my diary I'd already said I had blond hair and written that scene where the wind ruffles it. I liked all this. Later I peroxided my hair and became a bona fide blonde. This is how the era of lies and diary-writing began.

I reveled in my literary maneuvers, stole from books when I couldn't find the right words, and fabricated facts and experiences. But the diary was perfect. Almost as good as Laura Palmer's. In fact, I copied one of her entries in its entirety. It fit my situation: a big, evil grown-up who tortures me, wants to kill me. That was all true. In my life there was a big, evil grown-up who murdered my childhood: my mom's second husband, my second stepfather. But I was too scared to write about him directly. I couldn't imagine some future biographers finding my diary and reading the whole truth about what that man did to me. No! No! No! Anything but that! I was incapable of that kind of openness. I'd rather my future biographers read snippets of Laura Palmer's diary.

That's why I also lied shamelessly about my "first time." I described my first sexual encounter in detail, using metaphors from *The French Love Potion* and *A Slave of Love*. I reveled in romanticizing, even demonizing myself as a femme fatale. None of this had any connection to me or to my "first time." In the diary there was someone else, and it was all consensual, unhurried, and sweet.

Basically, the diary entry wasn't humiliating—it was nice. Elevating the reader, you might say, to the heights of goodness and love. An alternate reality, a sweet dream, not a word of harsh truth.

A few days later, on account of Murphy's Law, my mom read my diary. Standing over a batch of uncooked pelmeni in the kitchen, she randomly struck up a conversation about what happens between a man and a woman when they love each other, blah blah blah . . . I realized right away that she'd read my diary and I cornered her. She confessed, "Yes, I read it. I have to ask— is it true? You're not a virgin anymore? You're really dating that good-looking boy you wrote about?" (Sasha Shipulin) "Yes," I replied, "it's all true." We shed a few tears over my lost innocence. I said I wanted to marry him and my mom approved (which was weird, because I was fourteen). She clearly realized that I was mature enough, especially since I'd said so on the first page of my diary.

After moonlighting as a young bride-to-be who'd succumbed to love and passion, I went to my room, locked the door, and started rereading my diary. No, it's all good. I didn't give anything away. Not a word of truth. Phew.

What would have happened to my mom if I'd written the truth? I really wonder. Would she have killed him? Me? Herself? Gone crazy? Become a religious nut? Cried? Stopped loving me?

Or maybe she would've protected me? Hugged me? Taken me far away? Hidden me? No, not likely. Doubtful.

Just imagining what would have happened if my mom had found out the truth . . . it's unbearable. Why, though? It's all in the past! Water under the bridge! I was wise and cunning. I knew that, sooner or later, a reader would arrive on the scene, and I wanted to make a good impression.

I got a little carried away.

After Shipulin broke up with me— well, he didn't break up with me, really, just stopped walking me to the bus, said he didn't feel like it anymore— for a humiliatingly long time I wrote him notes and called his house, chatting with his mom for hours about her problems. I even went over to see her, hoping to catch Shipulin, but he never showed up. I couldn't write about how I was unsuccessfully stalking Shipulin, so I spruced up the story: "Fate has separated us . . . But I'll always remember you, my angel! The impossibility of touching you drives me crazy. You're so close, gazing at me again with those dark eyes [though his eyes were actually blue], and I know you want to tell me something. Quiet! Hush! Don't say anything. We are victims of fate. I know you suffer as much as I . . ." and so on. You get the idea. In the diary, I didn't give a reason for our separation. That bothered me. My reader would never forgive such a blind spot. So then I wrote, "I'm dying. They told me it's leukemia. I forgive you, I'm letting you go. You don't have to love me. Be happy. They gave me two years to live, and I will love you to my very last breath."

I really liked illness as a backstory. It explained everything, and I came off all selfless and magnanimous. I even wanted other people to know about my illness. For some reason I told Marina that I had two years left to live. And Marina told Sasha Shipulin. Sasha

Shipulin lost his shit and told his mom. His mom lost *her* shit and called my mom. That was it. I was fucked.

I remember it to this day, like a scene from a movie. The road, lined with pyramid poplars, extends to the sky. Then, a solar eclipse: everything goes yellow and red. I'm walking down the road and my mom runs toward me, wringing her hands and crying. She's just heard about the leukemia. Ambling up behind her is Shipulin—oh, God! I finally got through to him! Shipulin!

The weirdest part of this story is that my mom never took me to the doctor. She only asked how I found out I was sick. I thought of an answer on the spot: at my checkup they'd taken a blood sample, and the nurse who did the tests said that I had leukemia. This explanation was enough for my mother. Bless her heart . . . she didn't question for a second whether nurses are allowed to give diagnoses.

This is what happened. They decided to take me to this healer in Adygea for treatment. It took half a day to get there, to this healer's place. We all went: me, my mom, Shipulin, and his mom. Once we arrived, we waited a long time in the courtyard. I sat there looking tragic and helpless, like someone with an intimate understanding of life and death. The healer came out and started waving her hands over me. What's the problem? she asked. Our two moms answered in unison: she has blood cancer! The lady immediately confirmed this: yes, the child has blood cancer, that's right. Ten sessions. It'll cost a few thousand [I don't remember how much she said]. And the cancer will be gone. Both moms jumped for joy. Mine reached for her wallet.

Then the best thing happened: they made Shipulin come with me to my ten appointments. And he did. It was indescribably good. But all good things must come to an end. We went as a foursome to the tenth appointment, and the lady swore that the cancer was cured. To check, we could get tests done. Why didn't my mother get me tested before paying the lady??? Whatever, her total stupidity was in my interest: I'd gotten Shipulin for a while. Of course, when the tests came back, I was cancer-free. Oh, happy day! Champagne! Tears of joy! Our moms got drunk and sang drinking songs, while Shipulin and I sat across from each other and smiled reassuringly. But right after the celebration, Shipulin dumped me for the second time. And I didn't write about that in my diary at all.

Instead, I took pleasure in

describing the general qualities of love, death, partings, merciless fate, dreams, veins and blades, voyages, beauty, and eternity. Imagined relationships and adventures. In my diary I was always sassy, proud, and forbidding. But there wasn't a single description of an event that actually happened. I wrote: "The drums fell silent, the hum of voices turned into a heartbreaking wail. I quietly howled into the wreckage of my happiness. A black butterfly landed on my shoulder, fires reddened the horizon. I must go . . ." and so on. This abstract bullshit bore no relation to reality, and it filled up my entire diary. Three notebooks, in fact.

Once, I took out a separate sheet and wrote this clumsy passage: "Save me, somebody save me. Make him drop dead. I wish he were dead, I wish he'd get hit by a train. I wish his fucking house would burn down, with him in it. When I grow up, I'm gonna kill him. I'll kill him, Mother, no matter how much you cry. Goddamn fucking Uncle Sasha and my goddamn mother!"

I stuffed this sheet into the back of my dresser, back with all my school notebooks. But one day, when I got home, I saw my mom rummaging through that dresser. I stopped dead in my tracks and finally understood the phrase *my hair stood on end*. She'd ALREADY READ IT? And she was looking for more? I couldn't see her face, only her back and hands. Her hands were moving quickly. I was scared to call out to her, I thought that if she turned around and looked at me, already having discovered the existence of this sheet of paper, I would die on the spot. But I had nothing to fear: my mom finally grabbed some stupid magazine about knitting from the dresser and started furiously studying it. I went limp. That night I tore the sheet of paper into little pieces.

After that, my interest in writing fell off. I found a different kind of salvation: a real, long-term, serious relationship with a guy. I started spending the night at his place as often as possible, even though I didn't love him.

Before long, I went off to university. I got a job in TV. Then I got married. None of this went into the diary. Still scarred, I had stopped writing for three years, but then I couldn't help myself. I took the diary off its shelf and decided to reread it. I was horrified. On the cover, I'd written: "Diary with Exceptional Contents." As if. That night, I drank a can of Ochakovo gin and tonic, tucked the diary under my arm, and went out to the yard to teach it a lesson. I made a fire and gave the pages of my so-called life a nice toss into the flames.

My friend gave me a notebook with thin papyrus paper for my birthday. When I saw it, my heart skipped a beat. It was perfect for a diary. Not a word of lies in this notebook! I bought another gin and tonic, locked myself in my room, and opened the papyrus notebook. The whole truth and nothing but the truth. Right. I strained myself, trying to figure out what was especially important to me in that moment. Any minute now. I looked around my room. I wrote: "I need to disappear from here. Forever! None of this is *me*. Everything around here makes me sick. Weddings, kids, dogs . . . it's not *me*. If I don't get out soon, I'll die of longing."

There I went again, trying to write all sophisticated. I paused for a moment of self-reflection. Look at this bitch with her literary flourishes! Is it really so hard to write like a normal person? Whatever, to hell with it. At least it was true. True? I checked with myself. Yes, it was true. I really felt this way.

I continued:

> *Tonight I walked through my yard, where, as a kid, I did my best to make sense of the world. I realized that I've changed a lot. I've changed completely. The yard hasn't changed nearly as much. It will give other kids their own sorts of childhoods. I've really hardened, but I've also become more sensitive. I look at my reflection in the window, the new plastic windows in my horrible room, which I hate so much. People say that your childhood room retains your*

innocence, your original purity.
Mine is skeevy, dusty, and mute.
It's hiding shame. I look at
myself in the window and think,
I don't have a home. *Technically*
I do—it's right here, I was born
here, and I grew up here. I'm
registered at this address, so are
my mother and her newest hus-
band, who, by the way, are fuck-
ing in the other room. And that
fucker Uncle Sasha? He actu-
ally did die in a house fire. His
killer finally turned up. Thank
God it wasn't me. Thank God.
I go to the hot, gross-smelling
kitchen and pour myself some
water. I guess this is my home. I
know every splinter and creak in
the floor. But I have no feelings
toward it. This isn't really my
home. So what is? I often feel a

vague homesickness. But where home is, I don't know. When will I find it? What will it be like? I have to leave this city, where everything reminds me what a weak loser I am. I have to leave this city, this house, this yard, these people, my mother, my husband, my friends. I can't love anyone here anymore. I can't deal with this anymore. No one can stop me.

I exhaled and reread this. Was it true? Yeah.

"I'm an asshole. I don't like people. I don't know what you see in me, I don't understand why all of you tied me down and forced me to live with you. Why do you love me, my so-called loved ones?" I reread it. All of it was true.

I fell asleep, almost happy. But

then Murphy's Law struck again. My mom found my diary and, like before, she read it. This time, she didn't comment on it, she just took it to her sister's, my aunt's house, in the next town over. That evening they read it, reread it, and cried. My aunt drank vodka and my mom took Corvalol. Apparently they talked about how, despite having parents and relatives who were really very decent, I had turned out to be such a cruel and ungrateful bitch.

My aunt summoned me to a café to talk, ordering us both cognac. Then she was like, cut it out with the literary exhibitionism. Maybe you got drunk and felt like writing, but think of your mother.

Thinking of my mother was the last thing I wanted to do in that moment. I've been thinking of my mother my whole life, but right then I couldn't.

My mom agonized over this for a while, she screamed, saying I couldn't leave like this. Didn't I love her, my own mother?

I didn't know. All I knew was that unless I left, I'd start hating her.

She screamed that I couldn't leave my husband, my job, and her. I was her youngest daughter, by all accounts it was my job to stay close to her. I couldn't behave this way.

Turns out, I could.

Leaving for Moscow meant steamrolling over lots of people's feelings. But it didn't bother me. Not anymore.

Secrets

MY PARENTS GOT DIVORCED WHEN I was five. That's why I remember my father as a father only very hazily. I have a few memories. The first: I'm standing in the mudroom dressed in my winter clothes, ready to go outside, and I see my mom screaming hysterically, her arms raised, my two older sisters clinging to her like branches to a tree. My father's standing in the doorway, saying something like, "Oh, come on, Katya!" That was a weird moment. The second: my father is sitting on the couch, munching on sunflower seeds, and I'm on the floor by his legs, waiting for him to split some open and stick a handful of shelled kernels into my mouth. The third: my father asks me to bring him his slippers, and I say, "No, no, a nightingale never sings for a pig, ask a crow instead!" The fourth: I watch in horror as my father covers the kitchen floor with plucked chicken carcasses. The whole kitchen—the entire floor: carcasses. Nowhere to stand. As soon as he turns his back, I start frantically throwing the carcasses out the window, hoping I could still save them.

There you have it, all my memories. I'm not even sure they're real, they might just be imaginings based on my mom's stories.

Anyway, when I turned five, they got divorced, and I wasn't too upset because my mom, in celebration of her freedom, planned a nice trip to Taman and took me along. Sometimes I'd ask, "Mom, where's Dad?"

"What do we need Dad for?" she'd say cheerfully, bobbing in the sea, "We're having fun all by ourselves!"

I agreed—it wasn't bad without him around—and I stopped asking.

My father started living with another family pretty quickly, and soon there was a new girl calling him "Dad" without a twinge of conscience. None of it made sense anymore, and I stopped thinking of him as my father. I suddenly realized that being a dad was a bullshit temp job, that you could quit or pick a new daughter whenever you wanted.

My father loved my older sisters, but me, not so much. Probably because they were already wise and grown-up. They visited him a lot, but whenever I went, I just got fed and then sent home.

They always had the best chicken at his place. After the divorce, we never had chicken at my house. Clearly, my father considered it his sacred duty to feed me once a week. Soon, his new wife got sick of these feedings, and I could tell, so I stopped coming over for chicken. That's pretty much the whole story of our relationship, me and my father's. I didn't know him, never really had the chance.

My mom loved to sit me on her lap and ask, "Natashenka, what's your relationship like with Vitka?" That's what she called my father, short for Viktor. I'd say, "Well, what kind of relationship could I have with Vitka, since he got stingy with the chicken and gave me second-hand underwear for my birthday?"

"There," my mom finally said, satisfied, "you see! He's a pig! He's always been a pig! Now, I'm going to tell you something, but you can't tell anyone . . ."

Then she'd tell me some secret from their married life. My father had always been a horrible pig, he'd done some really awful things.

"Once," my mother said tragically, "Vitka lost some money to Polikarpych in a game of dominoes. To pay the debt, he said, 'Go to my place, Katerina will give you . . . well, she'll sleep with you.' So, Polikarpych came over, and I'm thinking, *Whoa whoa whoa, what's he doing here?* And he starts coming on to me! Right in front of you guys. But you weren't born yet. So, in front of Lena and Oksana. He started grabbing my breasts! I said, 'Have you lost your mind? Vitka will kill you!' But he said, 'Vitka's the one who sent me!' Well, I grabbed you kids and locked us all in the bathroom. He tried to force his way in but gave up after a while and, out of spite, locked us in from the outside. So we spent an entire day locked in the bathroom, hungry, with only tap water to drink. Then Vitka got home, unlocked the door, and told me to laugh it off!"

Wide-eyed with horror, I looked at my mom and thought to myself, *My father isn't just a pig, he's the ringleader of all the pigs in the world.*

God, Mom, no one asked for your fucking secrets!

But I understand how important it was for you to tell these stories. You needed an ally in that war. My older sisters were a lost cause—they loved their father. But I hadn't had the chance. That's how I became the Louise to my mom's Thelma. Even to this day. That's how intense and enduring these secrets have been.

Although now I realize how hard

that senseless marriage was on both of them.

Here's the story: My father had a girlfriend he was head over heels in love with. She cheated on him, or planned to, so he lost his mind and decided to teach her a lesson by marrying another woman. That other woman was my mother. That's it. When I asked my mom why she married him, she said, "Vitka was tall and handsome and, besides, I wasn't getting any younger."

The night before the wedding, my father's girlfriend called him in tears and begged him not to get married, to forgive her. But, like I said, my father had lost his mind. That's where stupidity gets you: married.

The wedding night didn't happen. He was drunk and rough and my mom screamed.

"That's when I realized what a mistake I'd made, Natasha!"

Really? Then why did you spend the next twenty years with him? Let's take a moment to process this: they didn't love each other for even a second. Not a single second.

Then he started cheating. Naturally, my mom was miserable. Why? Because they didn't love each other, of course!

But only now am I asking these questions. Back then, when my mom told me all this about her difficult fate, these things never occurred to me.

I didn't look like my father. Or my mother. I had tan skin. I was tall and thin, while my mom was short and curvy. I didn't look like anyone in my family. But my sister Lena also looked different—she had dark hair, and a mole on her forehead like a bindi. Only Oksana, my middle sister, looked like our mom.

Once, Lena pulled a stunt, a regular thing for her: she stole money and gold jewelry from her friend and made off for the coast with her fuck-buddy boyfriend. The friend came to see my mom and they spent a long time trying to get to the bottom of it. My mom was really worried that Lena had disgraced her again. It didn't take the girl long to realize she wasn't getting her money or jewelry back. She swore she'd beat the shit out of Lena and stopped coming over. Lena came back soon after, but my mom didn't let her through the door. "Get out," she said, "get out of here, I'll chase you out, go live on your own, since you're such a bitch." Lena went off somewhere (she came back soon, this time with a baby), and my mom, noticing how disturbed I was—how can you kick your own daughter out? That's crazy!—decided to share another secret with me.

"I raised you all the same, didn't I? And look what happened. Oksana is so sweet, and then there's this bitch! And do you know why? Do you? What do you think? You don't know? She's not my real daughter! I took Lena from the maternity ward! She's a gypsy! That's why she steals. There's no getting through to her! Well, she can go live with her band of gypsies, or whatever, for all I care!"

This secret was, as they say, a blow. It suddenly made sense why Lena didn't look like anyone in our family, why she had that pitchy hair, why she acted out so much, why she didn't value or respect our mother . . . But wait! I didn't look like my parents either! Did that mean I was adopted, too? And my secret hadn't been revealed yet because of my good behavior??? And as soon as

I pulled a stunt, my mom would say, "Well, of course—she's not one of us!"

Oksana was the only one who was clearly my mother's child, the spitting image. I compared photos of us as kids. Oksana was fair, with wavy light brown hair like my mom. She had sly green eyes and my mom's mouth. I was practically swarthy, a little puffy, with round eyes. No. We didn't look alike. Not at all. Not at all.

But I was scared of finding out the truth. My mom loved me, I knew it. Besides, finding another mom would be inconvenient.

I pulled stunts, as tests, but nothing happened, no secrets about my parentage surfaced. That meant my mom was my mom after all. Yay.

By the time I turned fourteen, I'd already forgotten about my fear of not being hers, and I'd come to terms with the fact that Lena was a gypsy bitch. By then all I thought about was boys and how to buy booze. I spent all my time squirming in front of the mirror, trying to make myself look better by popping my zits, combing my bangs, and bleaching my hair. I sang along to Tatyana Bulanova, she had this really sad song about her and her son, whose father had abandoned them.

So I'm standing in front of the mirror, wailing about this son, and my mom looks at me adoringly and then suddenly starts crying. I started asking her what was wrong. She asked me why I thought it was that I didn't look like her or my father.

I remember my insides were like: ba-boom, ba-boom, ba-booooom!!!

I'm thinking, *Fuck, this is it. Now she'll tell me that I'm an orphan and kick me out of the house. She kicked Lena out when she was around the same age. I'll have to find my real mother, Fuck, fuck, fuck!*

But she didn't say or do anything like that. This was a different secret. My father wasn't really my father at all. My real father was one of my mom's coworkers at the Institute of Animal Husbandry. They'd been having an affair for the past twenty years, and it was an open secret because our whole family had known for a while already, including my father, the one named Vitka.

My mom told me she'd decided she couldn't live like that anymore, with a pig for a husband. She'd wanted love and found it with this guy named Vladimir. He was married, of course, with two daughters ("Natashenka, I've seen pictures of them. You're the spitting image!

The spitting image!") and wasn't planning to get divorced. He and my mom had fun with their office romance, until she suddenly and foolishly decided she needed a child from him. She told him, and he carefully explained that it was her right, of course, but that it would be only her child, since he wasn't ready to leave his family. His wife was sick. I imagine my mother nodding happily: "I don't need anything, Volodenka, I don't need anything from you, just this child and some affection once in a while." Then they conceived me in some forest under the stars. My mom says that, straight afterward, she knew she was pregnant, and that's how it all started.

My father (Vitka) was thrilled when he found out my mom was pregnant. He already had two daughters, ten and twelve, and now he wanted a son. My mom also wanted a son (who looked like

Volodenka) and they happily started waiting for him (me).

Everything was fine, no one had to know, but my mother's happiness was so great that she couldn't wait to share it. Unable to find a more suitable candidate, she wrote a letter to someone she considered a friend: Vitka's sister in Ukraine. The letter contained a rich, literary description of her romance with Volodenka. She ended the letter by saying that she was expecting a son by Volodenka and her happiness was boundless. But Vitka's sister was, above all, Vitka's sister, which is why she stuck the letter in another envelope and sent it to him.

That's how the whole family found out my mom was knocked up. For a while, Daddy Vitka was regularly chasing Daddy Volodenka down with a knife. And my mom sobbed.

Daddy Volodenka decided to end the relationship with my mom for a while so that people at work wouldn't find out and tell his sick wife.

Daddy Vitka came to terms with it all and gave me his last name and patronymic.

Five years after I was born, they went through a painful divorce.

After hearing that story, I understood why my mom had been preparing me with stories of Vitka the Pig for so long. Because if I loved Vitka the Pig, and he loved me, then it would've been almost impossible to justify her passion for Volodenka to me. It was simple. Oh so simple.

Anyway, after my mom finished crying, I calmed her down, reassured her that I didn't blame her, that I forgave her, blah blah blah. She told me she wanted to arrange a get-together between me and Volodenka. I politely agreed, though I had no idea what Daddy Volodenka and I would talk about.

Then I decided to visit Daddy Vitka, the pig. I'd started feeling sorry for him. I bet he wasn't really such a pig. After all, he'd been generous enough to accept me as his own, to give me his name, even to feed me chicken and give me underwear. For the first time, I was ready to rehabilitate the other side. So I went to see Daddy Vitka. We sat in the kitchen and I ate something. His new daughter darted glances at me with jealousy and contempt for my tights, which were a little too small. Daddy Vitka asked me stuff like, are you spending time with any boys? Are you behaving yourself? I said, "I'm very well-behaved, I'm not spending time with boys, all I do is study, I'm planning on being a translator." After we ran out of things to say, I left, refusing the money he'd slipped into my pocket.

So I'd made peace with both my fathers, more or less. They weren't a part of my life and that was fine by me. At first, my mom kept trying to arrange meetings with Volodenka, but then she got busy and eventually stopped bothering.

Eight years passed. I didn't interact with either of my fathers, as usual. But one evening when my mom came home, her face looked old and gray. "Volodenka died. This woman at the store just told me!" My mom burst into tears, and I did too: sincere, bitter tears. I started feeling guilty that I hadn't wanted to meet him. My mother and I spent the entire night laying him to rest and getting drunk. I told her about the afterlife, not even believing my own words. She told me about his voice and his hands. We mourned him from the bottom of our hearts.

Then a few days later we learned that Volodenka was alive. The woman at the store was mistaken. He hadn't died—his mother had! He was alive and well. Raising his daughters, pitying his sick wife, business as usual.

Then my mom started planning our meeting in earnest. She gathered my best photos: me on TV, me in a play, me riding a horse. She went to see him at work. I waited impatiently for her to come back. At that point, after his burial and resurrection, I really wanted to see my father alive, while it was still possible. I imagined our meeting, how he would tell me, "I'm sorry, forgive me, I always knew about you, I have a photo of you from when you were six months old." And I would tell him, "Me too! I have a picture of you, too, Daddy Volodenka." That was true—I still have it. Basically, I needed to meet him to put this whole whirlwind with my fathers to rest and finally decide who to call Dad. But my mom came back downcast and pathetic. Here's what happened: Daddy Volodenka looked at the photos of me with interest and said polite things about the play and the horse but flatly refused to meet me. "Katya, honey, there's no need to dredge up the past. Let it be."

I think Volodenka was really just scared of Katya's desperation and her fondness for spilling secrets. He was also scared I would try to catch him up on the past twenty-plus years. I feel for him. It's not easy to get to know adult children.

My mom cried, and I spent a long time calming her down, assuring her

I wasn't mad, "I'm not upset, everything's fine, I keep his photo in my wallet anyway and kiss it at night. My dad is Volodenka and Vitka is a pig." Stuff like that.

A little while later, maybe three months, my mom called me and, like in a nightmare or an episode of *The Simpsons*, she repeated the news that Daddy Volodenka had died, only this time for real, from cancer. "It's over. Come home," she said, "we'll put him to rest."

I didn't go home. I could tell by her voice that she was fine. We'd mourned him well enough the first time. Neither of us needed a repeat.

Nothing flickered in me, not a drop of blood responded to the news. Maybe that was a good thing, maybe Volodenka was right: it's better not to know someone than to know them, love them, and lose them. It's less risky. Let it be, let it be . . .

No one asked for your fucking secrets, Mother.

Genes

"SIT STILL, DON'T FUCKIN' MOVE!" SHE
ties me to a chair with a scarf. My sister Lena, the gypsy bitch. Her fuck-
buddy boyfriend is over. They'll be in
her room for an hour or so, groping each
other. Then the boyfriend will want a
smoke and he'll step out to bum a cigarette. Once the groping's over, the par-
ty's over, at least in our apartment.

Lena knows I'm gonna sneak a
peek—all our doors have glass panes
in them. And though Lena's door is covered with a picture of some busty babes

on a motorcycle, there's a crack. It's easy to peek through and see the couch where Lena and her boyfriend are groping each other.

That's why, when her boyfriend comes over, Lena ties me to a chair with a scarf. No use resisting, you'll just get slapped in the face. I sit silently, doomed, fidgeting only because my arms hurt.

My mom's at work. Lena should be, too, but as usual she's playing hooky.

I'm sitting and thinking about how much I hate her. I started hating her pretty recently—right after I learned she's not my real sister, just a gypsy bitch.

My mom made this fateful mistake (adopting a gypsy bitch, I mean) in a moment of pity. I'm not sure who she was pitying—that putrid, screaming bundle or her own infertile self.

It happened after another still-birth. Doctors had been telling her for a while that she couldn't have children. No joke—one winter she fell into an ice hole up to her waist and stood in the freezing water for an hour. All her lady parts were frozen solid.

The doctors told her, "Ma'am, you can't have children, it's all chilled down there, fucking frozen over, your eggs just don't work." But my mom didn't give up. At first, she couldn't conceive, then she couldn't carry to term, then she couldn't birth them alive. And then, after the latest in a series of stillbirths, she roamed the hospital and masochistically wandered toward the screaming nursery. Well, there you go. She came across Lena, who wasn't even Lena yet, lying there in rumpled swaddling, unwanted. My mom went over and those little arms reached out to her.

In that moment, both their fates were sealed.

Any sentimentality my grandmother had ever had was long gone. The war, prison, and multiple rapes had left her completely jaded. She didn't believe for a second that Lena had reached her little arms out to my mother. She started poking around, looking into the baby's origins. And while my mom remained in blissful ignorance, snuggling the newborn like her own, my grandmother found out the baby's biological mother was a Moldovan gypsy, like the famous song, only worse, and Lena was already the second child she'd left in the maternity ward.

My grandmother screamed at my oblivious mom, saying genes always win out, there's no way you're adopting this gypsy baby. She'll be the curse of the family! But my mom just nodded and signed the papers. I'm adopting her. End of fucking story.

But, of course, my grandmother wasn't the only one against it. The whole family was twirling their fingers at their temples. Not only did the child look like a scary foreigner, she was also deathly ill.

In the maternity ward, Lena had been rotting in the most basic sense. My mom truly believed she'd saved Lena's life, and she was probably right. No one there cared whether Lena lived or died. They swaddled her at birth and never touched her again. If not for my mom, she would have rotted alive. It was Lena's lucky break.

My mom brought her home, gave her a bath, fed her some formula, dressed her, tended to her wounds, and that's how it all started. Vitka, her husband, either got used to it or didn't give a shit in the first place. He never held the baby. He was working a lot and playing dominoes.

Lena was quiet as a mouse. She entertained herself and never cried, just darted her black eyes, which peeked out beneath her jet-black hair. Even when she shit herself, she didn't cry, she just lay there quietly. Even when she was hungry, she just smacked her lips faintly and lay there, waiting, conserving her energy. Apparently, a genetic behavior—conserving energy for more important things. She was such an easy baby. My mom even went to the movies, leaving her home alone. Lena slept like the dead.

Everything was going well, but then my mom got scared. It all started when she dropped the bundle with Lena in it. It rolled down the stairs for a long time, long enough for my mom to assume the worst. She ran down to the bundle but didn't see a single teardrop or an ounce of fear. Not. An. Ounce. Those jet-black eyes were still calm. Then my mom really freaked out. She'd always believed in the Devil. The women at church had told her about children like this. The ones who don't cry or fear pain are the ones with the Devil in them. This thought kept my mom up at night. She even put Lena to sleep in another room. Like I said, she was really freaked out.

A few days later, to test her theory, my mom pinched Lena, hard. The baby squealed. There was a red mark on her skin. *Oh my God*, my mom thought, *she's a human being, for Chrissake*. And life went on.

Two years later my mom had a baby. A girl, a daughter, her very own flesh and blood. Fair, with light eyes and red cheeks, like a White Transparent apple. Cute little Oksana, her favorite.

This time when my mom left the hospital, there was an accordion player and bouquets of flowers. Lena and my grandmother waited at home. This celebratory parade, with a drunken Vitka at its head and all their family and friends behind him, burst into the house. Lena searched for my mom, spotted her, and rushed over. My mom bent down and happily showed Lena that pale, newborn face. For the first time in her life, Lena started crying, loudly and desperately. She was at that age—two and a half—when kids have their first crisis, that period of self-identification, and here comes this pasty-faced, rosy-mouthed, boob-sucking fucker to ruin everything. Lena wanted what she couldn't have—breastmilk—and she would jealously push that little white body off the boob and try to nurse herself. My mom was really taken aback. She's a big kid, she walks and talks, what does she need a boob for? My mom made short work of Lena's feeble cries for attention. So Lena tried to smother the bundle, but one of the adults saw and then laid into her with a willow switch, sealing Lena's hatred of her younger sister—that fresh little apple—for good.

They grew up as enemies. My mom spent a lot of time with Oksana, who was a nervous, sensitive, and shy child. She required a special approach. Oksana never left my mom's side, slept in her bed, and sat only on her lap. She was scared shitless of her sister. And she was right to be, because Lena had learned from a young age (or maybe she'd known since birth) how to set traps, frame people, take advantage, and steal.

My mother started spanking Lena when she was five years old, after she stole some processed cheese from the store. As time went on, the thefts became bigger, and the switches thicker. Seeing these regular whippings, Oksana tried to be as obedient as possible. Before my mom got home from work, she did all her homework, cleaned the house, did the dishes, brushed her hair, and practiced piano. The picture of a perfect child, the product of a proper upbringing.

Lena, though, devil that she was, started her day with a little school truancy, a cigarette around the corner, and then caught up on her sleep at home, not waking up until evening. Before my mom got home, she tried to make a mess wherever Oksana had just swept and mopped.

They fought. With glass, knives, and sticks. Lena usually won. Oksana left the battlefield with scars on her tender, pale body. The whistling of the switch started as soon as my mom got home. But it was no use.

"Genes! Genes!" my grandmother would say triumphantly.

By then my mom knew it was the genes, but there was no turning back.

Still, she tried to get through to Lena. She asked her teachers for help, but they were tired, stodgy women with a miserable lot in life. They couldn't help anyone anymore. And when, in seventh grade, Lena stole her teacher's wallet out of her purse, the teacher's council was relieved to kick her out. They didn't even let her finish the school year. What was the point? Lena had shown up only a handful of times that year. Was it really worth dealing with her until summer? They'd taught her how to read and write, that was enough.

And boy did she know how to write! Her greatest talent was forging handwriting and signatures. One time she wrote this note in my mom's hand-writing, something like, "Dear friends, I've fallen gravely ill, I urgently need money for treatment, as a loan, of course." With our mom's signature at the bottom. And then, like a profes-sional con artist, Lena showed this note to our mother's neighbors and acquaintances. They believed her. How could they not? They gave as much as they could spare. And then they were veeeery surprised to see my mom at the grocery store, alive and kicking. The secret didn't get out right away. Those nice acquaintances didn't want to be obnoxious, accusing my mom of lying and asking for their money back. They all thought, *well, you never know, maybe it's a silent killer, it happens.* But after almost a year, someone decided to hint at the debt. No surprise, my mom's face was blank—to her knowledge, she didn't owe any money.

My mom confronted Lena and made her tell how much money they still owed. But Lena had a strict rule: never tell the truth. In any situation, even in the deepest shit, she could tell only part of the truth, and in the most misleading way possible. So the truth surfaced gradually, over the course of a few more years. My mother still couldn't look people in the eye. Everyone seemed like a swindled creditor to her. But, kopeck by kopeck, the enormous debt was paid off.

Then I was born, and we went through a hard time. We really had nothing to eat. And, though Lena was skinny, she ate enough for three. She even ate baby food and powdered milk by the spoonful. My mom didn't have the strength left to raise three kids and nag Lena to go to work at the poultry farm. They fired her after two months when they caught her stealing chickens. She'd tucked their heads down and carried them under her skirt somehow. But her luck ran out one day when a chicken fell out at the guard's post.

"Genes!" my grandma screamed.

They tried to marry Lena off. To a foreigner. But what the fuck would a foreigner want with her? In the end, they couldn't get rid of her. The delinquency continued.

My grandmother couldn't hide her indignation any longer. She was ready to explode. The secret literally almost gave her a hernia. My mother couldn't tell Lena the truth, but my grandmother sure could. She'd open Lena's eyes, show her she was living here only out of the goodness of Katya's heart.

She found Lena and straight up told her she was an ungrateful bitch. "If Katya hadn't dragged you out of the shit she dragged you from, you'd have died a long time ago. Your biological mother left you, and Katya took you in like a puppy. You should fall to the ground and kiss her feet." Stuff like that. I remember Lena listening and saying nothing. She shrugged casually, as if none of it mattered. Not a living soul knows what happened to Lena after that conversation. We can only guess. Although, can we really? How could anyone imagine what it feels like to find out that the lady who's taken a switch to you isn't your mom, that your mother, your mama, your mom, your mommy . . . well, she ain't coming back.

Somehow, she found the strength to talk to my mother about it directly. She wanted to go look for her Moldovan gypsy mother, but my mom taunted her, stressed how impossible it would be. Lena cried a little, my mom calmed her down, and they were on good terms for a while.

But then we got some shocking news, a punch in the gut. Lena's best friend lost her mother. Lena went to help with the funeral and support her friend. And while the guests were paying tribute to the unexpectedly deceased, Lena snuck into the mother's bedroom and stole valuables from her jewelry box: her favorite gold earrings with rubies.

And then she came home as if nothing had happened.

The next day, Lena's friend came over in a fury, in search of justice. But Lena denied everything and cried big, bright tears. For some reason my mother bought it. How could she believe otherwise, that Lena had done such a horrible thing in the wake of her friend's incredible grief? Her friend, with whom she'd been joined at the hip? My mom told Lena's friend to look some more. The girl went home.

But a week later, in a very, very rare moment of diligence, my mom decided to do some cleaning up. And while changing Lena's sheets, in the corner of her pillowcase she felt . . . aha!

Our whole family got goosebumps. We respected death too much.

The family met and decided to kick the lying criminal out of the house. Those genes had expressed themselves in full. They'd taken the piss out of us. My mother nodded. She understood.

Lena was thrown out into the night, into the cold, told to go back where she came from. My mom didn't see her for over a year and didn't even care. Lena disappeared without a trace. Maybe she found the gypsies and they accepted her as their own, or maybe she died . . . who cares! The main thing was the peace and quiet that reigned in our house! My mom started singing day and night, feeling blessed. But getting rid of Lena wasn't in her cards. Finders keepers.

Lena turned up at our door not alone but with a one-month-old. My mom almost had a heart attack. She had no clue what to say, or, more important, how to remind Lena that she'd been kicked out.

My mom fussed over the baby while Lena drank some water from the tap, breathing heavily. My mom put them both to bed without any questions, but in the morning, she sat on the edge of Lena's bed and made her tell her story.

It's impossible to know what parts of this story are true, but here's how Lena told it:

When my mother kicked her out, for some reason she decided to hitch-hike to Cheboksary. Why? Why would you travel north (by our standard) in the winter? Unclear. Anyway, she did, and once she got there, she took up with someone and got pregnant. When my mom asked who the father was, Lena said she wasn't sure, there'd been a lot of them. Then what happened . . . well, the point is, she met these people, this infertile couple, who wanted to buy her baby. They came to an agreement and set Lena up in their house on the Volga, where she lived like a queen, any delicacy she asked for delivered posthaste. They pulled some strings to get her into a nice maternity hospital. Her obstetrician was one of the best. Lena gave birth—the baby just popped out, quick and easy. But when they brought the baby to her, Lena suddenly changed her mind. All of a sudden, for both the first and last time, she was seized with a maternal instinct. The sweet, sweet infertile couple from Cheboksary didn't insist on their part of the deal (they'd even paid her an advance, which Lena had already blown on booze). They didn't even ask for a refund for damages. This maternal instinct, though beyond their reach, was sacred. They respected every new mother's right to be seized by this instinct, regardless of any signed and sealed agreement. Basically, as usual, Lena got away with it. She was discharged from the hospital with baby Oleg Arturovich (not that she had any clue what his real patronymic was) and came home, where she was registered. "Well, here I am, Mom!"

Lena got tired of motherhood within a month. Her body was coursing with stronger instincts and they won out, of course. Plus, the baby had gotten really sick, probably picked up an infection on the way from Cheboksary. He had lots of problems, and Lena wasn't used to solving problems. She threw the violently coughing child at my mother and went on her merry way. My mom zealously took over Oleg's treatment, tended to him, and decided to seek the termination of Lena's parental rights so she could adopt Oleg as well. This was my mother's downfall: she loved nothing better than adopting people.

The whole family was up in arms. Someone said Katya should be forced into an insane asylum so she wouldn't be allowed to adopt Oleg. Everyone really liked this idea and started making plans, but my mom suddenly decided against adoption. Not because one of the relatives talked her out of it, but out of laziness. She couldn't handle, much less afford, all that legal red tape.

So things pretty much stayed the same.

I don't remember Oleg very well. I mostly remember him just lying there, hungry and dirty. Whenever he tried standing up and going somewhere, he got slapped with a fly swatter. Why? So he wouldn't bother the adults. Most of all, I remember Oleg sitting on the kitchen table. He sat like a frog, his dirty legs splayed out, eating meatless borscht straight from the pot with a ladle. Whenever my mom caught him doing this, she swore at him. The borscht was supposed to last the next three or four days, it was for *her* and *her* children. At that point, she'd crossed Lena off her list of children. Oleg, too. He kept guzzling borscht that wasn't his, although he couldn't have understood that at his age. Lena often polished off the contents of that very pot, standing on one skinny leg, like a heron, slurping from the ladle.

My mom was sick and tired of this.

The fridge migrated from the kitchen to the living room, which had been my parents' old bedroom, and was now the room my mom and I shared. A lock was set up on the door to this room. That's how my mom signaled to Lena that she couldn't mooch anymore. But Lena didn't give a fuck. She could mooch elsewhere. She spent the night with friends, hookups, and randos. They fed her dinner and breakfast. But that wasn't an option for Oleg. So my mom set aside one precious portion of *her* family's borscht just to keep Oleg alive.

This made things a lot worse between my mother and Lena. They were nasty to each other. Once, my

mom got up at night to go to the bathroom, and on the way she had a heart
attack. She fell down in the hallway
and lay there for a long time, unable to
call for help. And then Lena got up to
get some water, bumped into my mom,
stepped over her, drank some water,
stepped back over her, and went to her
room. My mom picked herself up somehow and then spent the whole morning
sitting in the kitchen, thinking.

Lena couldn't be thrown out, since
she and Oleg were both registered at the
house. And Lena knew she had a right to
be there. But living in such close quar-
ters, with Lena stealing everything that
wasn't hidden, insulting everyone, fucking practically in front of the children . . .
it was unbearable. My mother was nour-
ishing a viper in her bosom. What to do?

She started throwing around the
idea of a hitman.

I'm not joking. It was the nineties, and finding an affordable hitman was a piece of cake. She and my stepfather even started looking. I remember snippets of their conversations—just take her out with a gun and call it a day. They didn't say anything about Oleg. Maybe they were planning to spare him and put him up for adoption? Or adopt him themselves?

But those plans never went anywhere. To everyone's delight, Lena decided to get married. Yay. The guy was named Andrei, a total wimp. No one knew how Lena scored him. But what did we care! The important thing was that Andrei had his own place. OK, he shared it with his parents, but still, he had a place, somewhere to bring his new bride. Plus—and this really added to his appeal—he was from the city and didn't want to live with Lena in our little town. Yay!

After the wedding, Lena and Oleg moved out.

Within a couple of years, Lena had given birth to two more boys, one after the other. And then Oleg went missing. No use asking Lena about it, she gave a different answer every time. She said Andrei thought Oleg was an eyesore, and that Oleg had even started stealing from Andrei's wallet.

Genes, my mother thought to herself.

So basically, to hear Lena tell it, Oleg ran away after Andrei beat him to a pulp.

Another time, Lena said they threw Oleg out because he'd stolen her mother-in-law's watch. Lena's third explanation was that he'd gone to live with a friend for a while.

I'm pretty sure none of these excuses were true. But no matter what she said, Lena never tried to look for her son.

My mom got the police involved. But they searched for Oleg so . . . passively. "We're looking, we're looking," they said, but it was like they didn't even want to find him.

My mom had suffered enough at the hands of these genes. She deserved a break. Lena was worried her marriage was falling apart, so the disappearance of her oldest son wasn't exactly bad news.

It turns out no one wanted Oleg except that infertile couple from Cheboksary. They probably could've made his life bearable. But now they were gone and, besides, they wouldn't take a problem child who'd known only hatred, fear, hunger, and family betrayal.

I think it would've been easier for everyone if Oleg had never turned up. Maybe even better for Oleg himself . . .

But it turns out the police knew what they were doing!

They found Oleg about six months after he'd gone missing. He'd been in some detention center for a long time, he had memory problems, remembered only his first and last name. At one point, his memory offered up my mother's address, and the social workers rushed over. My mom and a police officer picked him up and brought him home.

He was terrifying. Scrawny, unwashed, covered in scabies, with scars and hematomas on his head. My mother wept as she washed him, naturally. She called Lena. "Keep him," said Lena indifferently. "Because otherwise Andrei will kick us all out and we'll come to live with you in your town, this time not two, but four!" My mom was really scared Lena's marriage was in jeopardy.

Oleg had to stay.

I took him to school and my mom watched him at home. But Oleg's brain was clearly messed up, really messed up. He was very good-looking and charming, but totally unable to do anything. Couldn't keep a job, couldn't do anything helpful. He was a carbon copy of Lena. Her exact copy. His only talents were lying and stealing. With talents like those, his path in life was clear.

He ransacked our apartment and ran away on three separate occasions. Later he would turn up in some shelter. And then my mom would bring him home, if only to preserve Lena's marriage.

Then Oleg went to jail for stealing a car. After that he went downhill fast.

When he wasn't in prison, he invariably showed up at my mom's door. The way back to her apartment must have been buried deep in his memory, since he had no other home. My mother would be scared stupid, shaking all over. She wouldn't open the door, she'd just lie in bed all night, trembling. He would ring the doorbell persistently and violently whisper: "Open up, Grandma, it's Oleg, I won't steal anymore, I'll never steal again, I love you so much, Grandma . . ."

These were his go-to lines, and my mom believed him every time. She let him in and tried to instill integrity, love, and a work ethic in him, but there was no room for those things with those genes. By this point she didn't believe him anymore. Besides, Oleg—whose brains had been scrambled since child-hood—didn't even belong to himself, clearly some greater power was in con-trol, values didn't stand a chance. He didn't have any. Oleg had never had a single value, ever since the days of the fly swatter and the borscht. He didn't even value his own life, didn't have an instinct for self-preservation. One desire ruled him completely: to take, to take what didn't belong to him, because nothing had ever belonged to him. To take, even for just a moment, to steal a car and go for a joyride with a girl who'd fallen for his shameless bright blue eyes and the smell of adventure, until he pulled up to the first traffic police checkpoint and went to jail for two years, then get out and steal something else, someone's money, to treat a girl to some champagne, because he couldn't even imagine a crazier splurge. All for that one moment when someone, anyone, looked at him adoringly and lovingly, maybe just looked at him at all, looked into those bright blue eyes. He didn't need anything else. That's all he ever wanted.

My mom and I were coming home from visiting friends. I was pregnant and going back to Moscow the next day. I was approaching the fifth floor, ahead of my mother as usual, since she had a hard time with the stairs. Someone was lying by our door. I called out to my mom, who was still crawling to the fourth floor. "Some drunk guy is lying here," I said. My mom froze, her voice changed, dull and morbid. "That's Oleg," she said. I didn't see her face, but I knew it was disfigured with fear. I looked at the man lying there. He was skinny, dark, and small. It wasn't Oleg. I remembered Oleg being tall, with clear eyes and curly hair. This guy was TOTALLY different. I told my mom it wasn't him. This was a migrant worker or something. She slowly reached the fifth floor, bent down over him, and repeated in that same dull voice that it was him. I couldn't believe it. I never would've recognized him.

My mom and I started tiptoeing around awkwardly, unsure what to do. She was scared that I'd get overexcited while pregnant. I was worried about her heart. I whispered that we needed to go inside quietly and pretend we weren't home. We stepped over him, the way Lena had once stepped over my mother. We didn't know whether he was alive or dead, drunk or sober, or really anything at all, and we didn't care. The person lying at our door was a total stranger to us.

We snuck into our apartment quietly, without waking him up. We lay in bed together for a long time, listening for sounds at the door. I asked my mom, "Where did he come from?"

She said he'd probably just gotten out of prison. I asked whether she wanted to call Lena. My mom said that if she called, Lena would just yell at her.

My mom said her one dream was to move away, so none of our relatives knew where she was, and to die there in peace, without any Olegs to worry about.

My mom said she'd never loved Lena. Apparently, she'd known right off how much unhappiness that child would bring.

My mom said she'd never get rid of this curse.

I asked her, "What would it be like if you loved Lena without giving a fuck, without a sense of charity, without expectations?"

My mom was offended. She said she'd raised us all the same. The same. "How am I to blame here? I raised you all the same. It's the genes, that's all. You can't get around them."

Then we went to sleep.

At three in the morning a violent knocking started. Oleg.

We didn't open the door.

He left at dawn. Who knows where to? I mean, this was his home, he was registered here. Although he had no way to prove it—no passport, no papers at all. Even if he'd had a passport, he'd never convince anyone that the bright-eyed guy in the photo was him, Oleg Arturovich Meshchaninov. Even his own mother wouldn't recognize him, and is that any surprise?

Desire

I MAKE A WISH ON A STRAWBERRY.

On a plane's contrails.

On a star.

On a wave.

I wish he'd get hit by a tram.

I was always afraid of the dead. But I liked his corpse. Not that I liked the corpse itself, but the image, him lying there dead, never to stand up again . . . What a heartwarming sight.

We're in a traffic jam, it's hot, there's a commotion ahead. We hear that some woman was cut in half by a tram. Our bus slowly approaches the place where it happened, and I see a piece of her leg sticking out from under the tram. Seeing it excites me. Excites my imagination. For a minute, I imagine it's his leg. My heart starts pounding gleefully. A few moments, then . . . ugh! It's over. He's alive again, sitting here, healthy as a horse. He's bugging my mom, saying we should walk instead.

Uncle Sasha, my stepfather. The second of my four stepfathers. And the most memorable.

He was small, shorter than me and even shorter than my mother, who was practically a dwarf. He was catastrophically thin, the result of polio.

A nimble neurotic. A violent psychopath. A pathetic little fucker. Yes. A pathetic little fucker.

I swim past him. He can't really swim, poor half-dead rat. As I swim by, my mom grabs me by the ankle and starts washing me with dish soap. She washes my greasy little head. All three of us are up to our waists in the stinky Anapka River. If you swim five minutes downstream, you'll reach the sea. The river flows into the Black Sea, where there are waves, sand, kids, and people. But we're here. We're here, scrubbing ourselves with dish soap and washing our underwear. We're here, taking pictures in front of the reeds and eating tomatoes with salt.

Why are we here and not, oh, I don't know . . . at the beach?

Well, because Uncle Sasha is ashamed of his skinny arms. He's ashamed of his skinny legs. For Uncle Sasha, the public beach is torture. He goes on vacation just to stand up to his waist in the river, not taking off his shirt (apparently his arms were worse than his legs; I never saw him without his shirt, although I saw him without his pants), and snicker at the people sailing by on catamarans, who'd pissed away all their money to sail on the stinking Anapka, when the beach was barely a hundred meters away. A man of contradictions, that Uncle Sasha.

We came here on vacation, but in the mornings, we work on a vineyard and in the evenings, we bathe with dish soap.

"Mom, what if Uncle Sasha stayed here and washed his hair, and we went to the beach? Can we?"

"Shh, what are you talking about, be quiet, go, go on, go play."

My mother is scared of Uncle Sasha. He'd gone psycho and thrown wood-carving knives at her a couple of times and she was afraid of provoking him.

Wood carving is what brought them together. Back then she didn't know that he would pitch knives at her and that they would break the skin. They didn't go in that deep, not really, they were specially made, short, thick, they could go in only a few millimeters. You could cut veins with them, or a throat if worse came to worst.

He and my mom carved linden wood with those knives. They collaborated on a piece to sell to foreigners: a trinket box that looked like St. Basil's Cathedral. Every cupola opened and there were two lower compartments as well. They stained it and painted the cupolas gold, and while they were working, they got together and decided to move in.

They had a place in mind: my mother had a two-bedroom apartment, while he had a whole house with a yard and a garden. The height of luxury.

Just take care of the garden and pick the cherries off the branch in time.

Uncle Sasha was obsessed with agriculture, so my mom also became obsessed with it. This came naturally to her, merging with a man into one whole and taking up his burning passions like they were her own. So they burned together. Hectares of potatoes and strawberries, endless patches of cucumbers and tomatoes, with raspberries and currants along the fence. A fruit orchard. Their own land wasn't enough for them, so they also started weeding sugar beet fields. Kilometers of sugar beets that needed to be weeded every other day. In return, we got a sack of sugar at the end of the summer. And then in the fall, we had to go to the beach and work on a vineyard. What a deal—we live in a trailer for free, gorge on grapes by the bucketful, and even make money on top of that. Harvest in the morning, swim at the beach in the evening.

But we didn't go to the beach. Sometimes I felt like Uncle Sasha made sure I never got anything for free. That anything good came at a price.

The price?

Love for Uncle Sasha.

I make a wish on a rainbow.

On thunder.

While sitting between two girls named Olesya.

On the spring equinox.

I wish he'd fall off a cliff and get picked apart by flies.

I hide from Uncle Sasha in the vineyard. He's looking for me, already annoyed. Soon he'll get so mad that I risk losing not just the beach, but also my next two meals. But I can handle it, I really can, just as long as he doesn't find me here . . . The sun just set behind the mountain. Uncle Sasha should go back soon, too. My mother made potatoes with lard, before long she'll come out into the trembling valley to look for us both. She thinks we're playing. No, Mother, we're not playing. Uncle Sasha is hunting. I'm breathing shallowly, sensing how much stronger and more brutal he is than me, for all his feebleness.

He doesn't find me. Yay. My mother comes out to the vineyard looking for us. I run up to her and she sees me, so today Uncle Sasha will leave without his prey. For that, I'll pay a steep price.

"You're eating like a pig. I told you to take the bread with two fingers, not with your whole hand."

It's starting. Now he'll find a reason to take my food away.

"Your mother gave you too much. Look at my plate and then look at yours."

He takes my whole plate of potatoes and slides half onto his own plate.

In a timid voice, my mom says, "Sasha, you know she has a healthy appetite."

"She doesn't have an appetite, she has a tapeworm. Appetite, my ass! Take some more bread, but with two fingers, two!"

I focus on the bread and forget about my fork with an impaled potato on the end. I make an awkward movement and the potato flies onto my bare, tanned lap. Uncle Sasha peers down way too intently. My mother might have noticed something was up if she'd seen that look, but she was busy slicing bread.

After running his eyes over my lap, Uncle Sasha cinches his victory: "I can't eat with pigs. Leave."

I don't say anything. Neither does my mom.

"Do I have to repeat myself?"

My mother stares wide-eyed at me. I leave the table.

I pick up a walking stick and go into the dark vineyard. Crickets are chirping desperately, and mosquitoes are flying around in swarms. I start tearing down grape branches furiously with my stick. I hate the grapes, I hate them. Two more weeks here, two more weeks of eating them for breakfast and lunch, with garlic and lard as snacks. I think about how when I grow up, I'll start by killing Uncle Sasha and then I'll never go near another grape or ounce of lard.

When I get back to the trailer, my mother and Uncle Sasha are inside, messing around quietly. On the table outside the trailer, there are three dirty plates. My potatoes are gone. I sit on the trailer's steps for a while, breathing in the air from the faraway beach, which is so hard for me to get to, and I dream about running away at night. Before long my mother comes out of the trailer, happy. She starts washing the dishes in the dirty basin. I don't even ask if there are any potatoes left over. I know there aren't. I'm thirsty. I tell her, "Mom, I'm thirsty."

It's dark as we walk to the public bathroom, but there's no water there, the tap has been turned off.

"There's no water, the tap has been turned off," my mother says serenely.

I have to wait until morning, but I don't have the strength. I'm not just thirsty, I'm dying of thirst. I understand how people in the desert must feel. And, come to think of it, I am a person in the desert. I go and drink greedily, without wincing, from the dirty basin where my mother washed dishes all day. I'm a desert warrior. I'll take whatever water I can get.

Somewhere over by the bathroom, my mother starts singing:

"We have mountains, we have plains,

We have windiness and wilderness.

We are children of the stars

But more than any other,

We belong to you, we're yours,

The eaaaaaarth is our mooooother."

The mountain edges have blurred with the sky. You can't make anything out in the dark, there aren't even stars. Tomorrow will probably be cool and overcast.

I sink onto the mattress on the floor of our trailer. My mother and Uncle Sasha are in the bed next to me. The springs keep sagging violently beneath them. They're messing around again, thinking I'm asleep. I'm not asleep. I hear my mother whisper this long, hot string of vowels, and also his shallow, mouselike breathing.

He didn't catch me in the vineyard, which means my mother will be satisfied tonight.

I'm scared of telling her. Scared. Scared to even hint at it. I feel so bad that I'm like this. I feel so bad that her husband, my stepfather, Uncle Sasha, is like this. I remember so well how she used to cry over him.

I was sitting on his scrawny, jittery knees, sensing his flaccid, sometimes twitching penis.

He forced me onto his lap while my mom was in the kitchen making potato pancakes. I heard the frying noises, but she didn't hear my desperate hissing.

Uncle Sasha had sat me on his sharp knees so I would tell him whether or not I'd like him to keep being my father.

Father?????

My father??????

I mean, the way I saw it, a father was someone who . . .

I'd never had a father.

I didn't know how it was supposed to be, how a father was supposed to talk to you, although . . . I definitely couldn't imagine a father wriggling my butt along his penis like it was the most normal thing in the world.

Anyway.

I worked up the courage to say, "Uncle Sasha, I'd like it if you'd fuck off somewhere far away."

It seemed like he was expecting this. Without another word, he let me off his lap. Later I found my mom in the garden, her face red from crying. He'd told her, "Listen, I can't be with you, your daughter hates me, she just told me, she wants us to break up . . ."

And, you know, so be it.

My mother rushed to the garden, waving her arms. She hugged a blossoming apple tree and cried. The stress hit her like a brick, that's how nervous she was imagining this worm would dump her.

But here's the kicker: the worm wasn't even planning to dump her. Why would he, when she had a growing grasshopper daughter? He was playing hard to get.

It worked like a charm.

My mom was mean to me, said I wanted to ruin their happiness. At dinner, Uncle Sasha was sad and tender toward her. She looked at him with the sad eyes of an abandoned woman. Luckily, my mother saw honor in the "abandoned woman" role.

I was the snake who wasn't even allowed to come to dinner.

Well-executed manipulation can really do wonders. Uncle Sasha's stock went up, and I was more humiliated than ever.

Later he told me I was a dirty, mangy cat, that only he had the power to save or destroy me.

I was his slave.

I worked in his fields, ruled by the slightest twitch of his hand or movement of his pupils.

He'd buy me Barbie and her boyfriend, Ken, sour cream, and leggings. If I let him catch me.

He was concerned with my education. He showed me magazines with didactic pictures of men and women fucking in different positions.

He said all this would help me improve my relations with my future husband.

He also controlled my love life.

I didn't have much of one at nine, but by thirteen my needs were growing.

Any relationship sounded good to me, as long as it was with someone my age. I had a fleeting hope that one of them would shove a wooden stake up Uncle Sasha's ass in a jealous rage.

But what options did I have at thirteen? Just dickheads with dirty, greasy hair, like me. They couldn't even whittle a wooden stake.

Uncle Sasha gave them honey from his apiary and watched their faces closely. They flushed, guzzled the honey, and made a run for it. They thought I had a strict father who wouldn't let them take any liberties. So at thirteen I was surrounded by a bunch of spineless, zit-faced honey-lovers. Thanks a lot, guys.

Uncle Sasha ruled over me completely, with impunity.

I make a wish on the first ray of sunlight.

On a raven's feather.

On poplar tree fluff.

On a crescent moon.

I wish the bees would sting his throat and he'd stop breathing.

In the summers we lived by daylight. To save electricity. For example, we weren't allowed to read with a light before bed. We couldn't do anything, really, even turn on the light to go to the bathroom. Because kilowatts really add up. We burned homemade candles whenever we had to do something after dark.

All this was because the sewing machine we used to make white cotton purses took so much electricity. Those purses were another source of income for our family.

We drove to Taman to sell them.

For some reason, people went crazy for this type of bag in Taman. We sold them without a license around the market. My mom and I stood at the corners and Uncle Sasha ran between us, overseeing the whole operation. He had an animal sense for when the people who ran the market were coming. A few minutes before they appeared, he would sense a stirring in the air and his thin lips would sharply tell us to pack up. His prophetic powers always scared me. My mother venerated them. She respected psychic abilities—tried to discover them in herself, and later in me, but only ever found them in Uncle Sasha.

Casually whistling, we hurried to close up shop. Then we swanned around, pretending we were incredibly interested in the Taman melons, all the while right under the market people's noses. Other vendors winked at us conspiratorially. Most of them liked our purses and were glad we were selling them there. No one gave us away. We always got off scot-free, like in some movie about professional scam artists.

I always thought of the market people as cartoon villains. It was easy and fun to run away from them. But I still didn't like selling those purses. Actually, I hated it. I wasn't any good at sales. I always did it wrong. I sucked at bargaining. So I'd sell three bags for next to nothing, all because the customer talked me into a profitable wholesale deal, but I wasn't willing to knock a kopeck off the price, even though the customer was already willing to buy one of the biggest, most expensive purses with my mom's embroidery on the front. Uncle Sasha would rage at me every time he came to check on my corner.

The way he saw it, I was so incompetent that all I was good for was satisfying him.

He tried to take me with him wherever he went. And he always tried to make my mother stay home on the pretext of her bad heart, or hot weather, or to cook and clean. Basically, Uncle Sasha had done pretty fucking well for himself. He essentially had two wives: an experienced one for urgent business, and another one, barely a fledgling, for thrills.

No matter where he and I wound up alone—weeding beets, picking wild apricots, in a ditch with a dog—he always seized the moment. Most of the time, there was a happy ending. I always cried when this happened, and afterward as well, but that only pleased him more. He was a pretty upbeat guy, in general. At least, I never saw him sad. He was upbeat and short-tempered. And for that, he was incredibly pitiful.

An upbeat, short-tempered, pitiful maggot.

My mother obviously found all these traits irresistible. She bowed down to them, as if to a god. Although she probably would've described these traits in different words, like "strong," "fair," and "psychic." I don't really know what she was thinking . . . Whenever I asked her, "Hey, how's it going with Uncle Sasha?" she always gave a hurried, kind of confused explanation. But there was never a mention of love when she talked about her feelings for him.

As for him, I think (though I never asked) he wouldn't have mentioned love if he'd tried explaining his feelings toward my mother or me. Especially not toward me.

Sometimes we got along, though. Or we had fun, at least. I did theater bits for him and my mom. Some dancing and singing numbers. I read them my childish stories about love, doing the different characters' voices. They sat in a "hammock" hung between two pear trees. It was made from a metal bed frame that looked like those old Soviet mesh shopping bags. They swayed back and forth, embracing, and I stood in front of them with a sheet draped over my shoulder like a Roman poet. Uncle Sasha got excited by this, and after my recitals he always tried to catch me. If I didn't turn up, the evening went to hell. Instant scandal: apparently while I'd been singing, dancing, and dicking around, the carrot patch hadn't been thinned, the tomatoes hadn't been watered, the floors hadn't been mopped, the fallen plums hadn't been collected, and the dog shit hadn't been picked up. My mom rushed off to make potatoes, tail between her legs, and I trudged away to pick up the dog shit and finish all the yardwork at dusk.

Uncle Sasha was way nicer the next morning. He'd laugh as he remembered my stories, smugly declaring that when I grew up, I'd write a serious story about him. Or a novel. And, by then an old man, he'd leaf through it while sitting by the fire, remembering me as a girl, a skinny little grasshopper scratching her mosquito-bitten calves.

When I imagined this, all I could think was: Uncle Sasha has to die before I can ever write stories like that.

And that's why I wished on every bug, every fallen leaf: somebody help, make him die!

I also wished someone would fall in love with me. I started wishing for that at ten. That's why Indian movies had a big effect on me. They always had a mean, pervy creep with an earring who shamelessly and skillfully unwound the innocent heroine's sari. But! In the nick of time, after giving the heroine time to cry, Mithun Chakraborty would show up. Handsome. Young. Scrappy. And at the same time, an unbelievably good guy. His victory was more symbolic than anything. He never killed the creep, just wrestled him to the ground.

I, for one, would've preferred a more bloodthirsty Mithun Chakraborty. Any day now, he'd come and pay a visit to Uncle Sasha. After falling in love with me, obviously. And then we'd have to run from the law and go abroad, hopefully to India. And we'd disappear into the beautiful Indian landscape.

Without my mother.

Let her visit Uncle Sasha's grave

and grow radishes there. Let her remember and begrudge me and Mithun Chakraborty for cruelly thrusting a stake up Uncle Sasha's ass and thus bringing him to an unsavory end. Let her cry. Let her. Let her tell the neighbors what kind of monstrosity (me) she brought into the world. Let her hate me, let her be enraged for no reason. As long as she doesn't know the truth! As long as she doesn't know! Let her cry, let her hate me, but let her live. Because if she finds out, or even guesses, she'll die on the spot. I had no doubt about it. Because that's something mothers can never survive. They just can't. There are some things they just can't survive. And this thing is definitely on the list.

I wish on whatever the fuck I see, on everything.

If only a huge earthquake would hit

us, grinding his village, his house, and him into dust.

In the rubble, my sobbing mother would find my nude photos.

The ones Uncle Sasha took when I was eleven.

In them, I'm lying naked, my skinny legs spread, trying to hide my face.

When I was fourteen, Uncle Sasha finally fucked me for real. After that, everything in my life lost meaning. Everything except Mithun Chakraborty. I waited desperately for him, looked for him in everyone I met: men, boys, and even girls. But the people I met didn't give a fuck about Uncle Sasha. Actually, in some mysterious way, they themselves were an extension of Uncle Sasha. They only wanted to fuck, had no intention of loving me. But I stubbornly kept looking, plunging my body into a mass of protruding dicks. There was nothing more disgusting than that. I didn't expect my search for Mithun Chakraborty to be so heinous.

By the way, my mom was still serenely oblivious. My lying didn't bother her at all. She easily believed whatever bullshit I offered up. She didn't worry, either, when I came home drunk at four in the morning stinking of cigarettes, covered with bite marks and hickies, with weed in my pocket and semen in my hair. The next morning, before I'd even had a chance to freshen up, she'd kiss me without a hint of embarrassment. Not a single obscene thought crept into her head, so innocent and pure was my mother.

She didn't even find the emo, dangerous guys who called our apartment past midnight worrisome. She opened the door good-naturedly and let them into our house, like friends. Your friends are here, she'd call to me. I'd hesitantly come out of my room and my "friends" would grab me by the neck and make me go out with them. "Mom, I'm going out," I'd squeak, and she wouldn't notice anything unusual in my voice. She never noticed anything about my situation in general.

In stripping me of my innocence, Uncle Sasha didn't realize that he wouldn't be the only one to travel that road. That there would be hikers fiercer than him, who'd only let me go home in the morning. My calendar was like one of those dance cards at a ball, and there wasn't a single line left for Uncle Sasha. And he couldn't make me cancel a dance with another partner, a young insolent guy. Not anymore. He'd been sidelined. But he wasn't about to give up. He started coming for me while I was asleep. Of course, reciprocity wasn't important to him. All he cared about was easy access. The best time was around five or six in the morning, when my sleep was super heavy from alcohol and exhaustion. I'd wake up to the unpleasantness of Uncle Sasha fumbling on top of me, lightly and quietly. And every time I saw him, and more importantly, felt him, I thought my lungs were filling with lead. But still, I was growing. And my lungs were expanding, too.

At seventeen, I suddenly realized I was physically stronger than him. I probably had been for a while, but I never felt I had the "moral" right to raise a hand against him.

But then I suddenly discovered that right.

It was pretty unexpected.

My mom was in the hospital after a heart attack. I was making soup to take to her.

Uncle Sasha prowled around me, getting ready to pounce. My mother's heart attack and her absence excited Uncle Sasha's thin blood.

When he came and pressed himself against me clumsily, I surprised even myself, as if I had some sort of super-power, when I fiercely threw his slight little body to the end of the hallway and he hit his head on a cabinet.

At first he was taken aback. Flustered, even. But after a minute he slipped away to the kitchen and grabbed a knife. His eyes were water-ing, he couldn't help it. It was awesome.

He stood across from me with the knife. I found the strength to laugh loudly. At him. At his polio. At his impotence. At his shrimpy body. At his temper. At his wormy wretchedness. At his lust and at his penis.

I laughed out loud. I told Uncle Sasha exactly what I was laughing at. I didn't give a fuck about the knife. I knew I was already killing him with my laughter. My young, powerful, cynical, fearless laughter. I realized he'd never been on the receiving end of this.

When I was done, basically when I got tired of laughing, I had to go see my mom. I walked right past him. And he was still holding the knife, staggering a little, like a child who can't walk without holding onto a grown-up's finger.

I walked by unobstructed. And, going for an offhand, imperious tone, I told Uncle Sasha to fuck off.

He better be long gone by the time I get back from the hospital.

My sick mother had other plans for Uncle Sasha. She begged him for

forgiveness, blamed me without trying to understand what had actually
happened.

He graciously stayed in the family.
Only now he tried to stay closer to my
mother and farther away from me.

I had a recurring dream where I
pricked his balls with a woodcarving
knife. But it's hard to control dreams,
so by the end he always managed to
gain the upper hand. He cut my tendons
with thin blades so I couldn't run, and
his hands clung to me even after I took
his life. Even after death, he could hold
me by the throat in a dark corner. He
was invincible.

I'm drinking and writing, drinking and writing, mixing champagne
and vodka. I'm on the train to Moscow,
writing a script, more like a synopsis,
that ends with me killing Uncle Sasha.
I spent a long time trying to figure out

how to do it, and then it came to me:
I thrust a screwdriver, a huge slotted
one, right under Uncle Sasha's Adam's
apple. I'm taller and stronger than
him. He shrivels like an oyster under
under lemon juice. He starts gurgling.
I rejoice. Finally, his corpse. The long-
awaited sight, almost like an icon—for
real, though. Uncle Sasha's corpse has
the same visual power for me as icon
paintings do for some people.

The train shakes as usual and I
drink champagne and vodka in the
same glass. I finish writing the finale
around five in the morning and then
settle down and sleep for two hours. By
eight we're already at Kazan Station.

January, snow, Christmastime.

I brought a small bag, like for an
overnight, but I'm actually moving here
for good. And even though I'll still pin-
ball between Moscow and Krasnodar,

soon there won't be a drop of Krasnodar blood left in me.

I left sixty-degree weather and arrive to a snowstorm outside, which I absolutely love. I'm kind of drunk and I like the way the snow is landing on the back of my neck. I could walk across the entire city without getting cold. I feel like I just successfully escaped the KGB cellar and got a face transplant.

No one knows me here! Not a single person! No one!

I smile as I walk. Everyone must think I'm adorable.

I meet people, get to know them, talk about stuff. No one assumes anything about me. They have no idea who I am.

It's intoxicating.

In Moscow, there wouldn't be— couldn't be—any scary village kids who knew I "put out." In Moscow, there wouldn't be—couldn't be—an Uncle Sasha, who always showed up unannounced in my life. Even after he and my mom got divorced, I'd sometimes find him in my childhood bed. Ugh. I guess whenever he asked to spend the night, the best my mother could come up with was to stick him in my bed.

But in Moscow, forget about it! I won't run into Uncle Sasha anywhere. Anywhere! His face and hands won't disturb my sleep anymore. It's over. It's all over.

I got some more alcohol and went over to my friends' place. They were busy with work, so I spent the evening on my own in their apartment. I loved drinking Coke and cognac and watching the snow.

Then my mom called me.

And with that typical intonation of hers, that voice grown hoarse with grief, she told me Uncle Sasha had been brutally killed that night with a screw-driver to the throat. The very same night when I was on the train writing about killing him. The very same screw-driver to the throat. Then, with no concern for my reaction to the news, my mom started talking about the funeral, about how she wanted to go and say goodbye to him. Then she talked about the suspect, some guy with an under-aged girlfriend Uncle Sasha had photo-graphed nude. The boyfriend had found out, gone crazy, and killed him. They'd known to go looking for the boyfriend after finding the girl's photos.

"Did they happen to find my photos, Mom?"

I really wanted to ask her that . . . but I just hung up.

Then I called my friend in Krasnodar, who was partly up to speed on the Uncle Sasha story. I roared into the phone hysterically about how I killed him dead with a stroke of my pen. My friend asked for details, all businesslike, but then, with her classic sense of humor, she asked me to write a few more synopses that ended with the deaths of her enemies. She had her own corpse-themed vision board. And she didn't doubt the power of my pen for a second.

I hung up again.

I wanted to write something really badly, but I was scared it would come true.

I was sure I had stronger psychic powers than Uncle Sasha. Killing some-one from a distance—now that's the big leagues. And that guy who physically thrust the screwdriver into his throat didn't even realize he was merely my pawn.

I felt like God.

I downed an unseemly amount of Coke and cognac and then lost myself in sleep.

I had to see the long-awaited corpse. So I went to Uncle Sasha's funeral.

Uncle Sasha's two daughters from another marriage were there. They looked at me with jealousy and dislike. My mom and aunt were there. Everyone was grieving and pretending they didn't know why someone had thrust a screwdriver into Uncle Sasha's throat.

I drank in the sight of his corpse.

It made me unbelievably happy. Rarely in life have I experienced such euphoria without drugs.

His throat was tactfully covered by a collar and some sort of shirt frill. I started wondering who had dressed him for his last journey . . .

My mother stood at the edge

of his grave, her face lowered. She seemed ready to jump in with the coffin. Uncle Sasha's daughters were huddled together. It was incredibly hard for me to hide my glee. Every strike of the hammer on a nail was like a song to me. A song. A song.

During the reception, my aunt and I went outside for a smoke. She said she wanted to talk to me before I went back to my precious Moscow.

Sure, of course. Let's talk.

She talked in circles for a while, about how she and my mother had talked a lot about Uncle Sasha after he died . . . about how it'd been, living with him . . . and this and that, blah blah blah . . .

And then she raised her heavy eyes at me and, exhaling smoke, sharply asked: "So did you seduce Uncle Sasha?"

While I tried to control my lungs,

what followed was a short and laconic speech. She and my mother had a simple explanation: the whole time Uncle Sasha and my mother lived together, I, like fucking Lolita, was seducing Uncle Sasha and he was cheating on my mother with me.

I wasn't particularly surprised, except by one thing. One thing that completely invalidated my sacrifice. My many years of silence. Just like that, my great idea of protecting my mother's heart was shot to hell.

My mom knew.

From the start. Since I was nine.

And she survived.

My mother's a survivor, all right.

She survived something mothers are never supposed to.

Mom

EVERY COMMENT, EVERY SENTENCE OF yours drives me fucking nuts.

But I'm sitting here, keeping a straight face, being patient.

In reality, I'm about a second away from bursting into tears at our incompatibility. I've been a millimeter away from that for years now.

We're sitting in a restaurant. I take you to a restaurant every time you visit me in Moscow. You expect an act of generosity; I come through. Actually, maybe you don't even expect it—but I come through.

I look at you. You've got a lump of potato salad on your fork and you're swaying to the beat of a song some random guy is performing live . . . He's singing especially for you, this Armenian singer. His voice is godawful. Unbearable.

But you're swaying, oblivious to how godawful this performance is.

The blood is draining from my ears, but you're A-OK.

I feel the urge to flip the table, but you've come for a week. I can survive a week without flipping tables, with some teeth-grinding.

Mom.

I love you.

I say this to myself once every minute, so I don't turn into a monster. I say these words—"I love you"— as if to absolve myself a little. I try to balance the scales unconsciously with these words.

"I love you, Mom." It's a spell that keeps me from turning into a werewolf when the sun goes down.

I close my eyes and remember how you smelled when I was a kid. I remember how I'd hug you and smell your pillows furiously whenever you had gone away. How I'd wait for you to come home from work and, after spotting you from the window, I'd start running around the room and singing. How I'd climb under the table at dinner. It was dark down there and I could only see your knees and I'd feel a surge of happiness, seeing them. I'd crawl under the table knowing your knees would be there with me. I remember your voice, your hands, rough from something, but still nice, when you used to stroke my hair hard. It hurt a little, I had sensitive, thin hair, but still. It made me happy that they were your hands, your hands, Mom.

Our conversations before we fell asleep, when—lo and behold—I ended up sleeping in your bed, and you told me about your job, about sheep and goats and ostriches. And how I'd squint with pleasure and fall asleep sweetly.

The way you adored me, worshipped me, when I worked myself into a frenzy and grimaced while doing impressions of Philipp Kirkorov, Kuzmin, all the performers you liked. When I put on ridiculous rags and you applauded me like a real fan: "A star is born! A star is born!" Your hugs so tight, your aggressive kisses, like in Soviet movies when they bruise each other's cheeks. Your presents: a Cinderella doll with a change of clothes and Karlsson, whom I always punished for disobedience—like you did me—with a willow switch from the tree that grew outside our window and always turned green before the other willows in spring . . .

I open my eyes. Now I have the strength to smile and speak with you more gently.

I preserve these feelings inside myself artificially, these feelings that I don't have the right to give up. That I don't want to lose.

But it doesn't last long. You'll say something stupid again and I'll explode. No one in the world can drive me over the edge like you.

We're sitting together in the kitchen and you say:

"You know, you're so fat, and I can't figure out why . . . We were all so skinny . . . I was skinny till I was forty. Everyone told me I looked like Thumbelina. I'm fat now, of course, but that's understandable. On the other hand, now that I'm fat, I look like Catherine the Great!

Me—Catherine the Great! I've always wanted to be Catherine the Great. In fact, as Empress Catherine the Great, I've brought the nice Krasnodar weather to Moscow. Otherwise you'd freeze here. But I brought warm weather. See?"

"You know, Leonid told me I should donate my *sarafan*. Honestly, it ages me. Nooooooo, Leonid doesn't know how old I am. Are you serious? God forbid! That's why I'll never call an ambulance, even if I'm in real trouble. The first words out of the lady's mouth will be, 'How old are you?' I don't *think* so . . . I'll never call an ambulance in front of Leonid. Besides, I've collected and dried so many herbs, they're like my very own ambulance. One time I took some aloe and honey and, to be fair, my body broke out in an allergic reaction and I ended up having to call an ambulance anyway . . . I have such a great aloe plant on my windowsill. If you come home, I'll cut some off for you, you can bring it back to Moscow and then you'll be healthy as a horse."

"You know, I bought you a sheep-skin coat, an extra-large. What? You won't wear it? But it's nice, look, so warm. It's brown, even. I remember you always liked brown suede jackets. What? Why are you yelling? Well, give it back . . . somebody will wear it. Calm down, I didn't waste my money. I didn't buy it. This woman gave it to me. You know her, she's nice, she's a poet, too."

"Did you know that St. Basil's Cathedral was built before Christ? But what does it say on Wikipedia? What is Wikipedia, anyway? Who cares what they write there! Ivan the Terrible? I'm so sure. It's a pagan temple, I'm tell-ing you, our ancestors built it before Moscow even existed. It's a pagan temple in honor of the god Ra! Seriously, that stuff on Wikipedia is horseshit! I'll give you a book to read, it's got the real story."

"Did you know that dolmens cure cancer? I know a woman who drank a calendula tincture and sat by a dolmen for three full months, and her cancer was cured. Do you get checked for cancer? I don't. I know what to do if something comes up. The dolmen cure. They cured a woman of sterility. People go there to jump over fires, too. But not close to the dolmens. You can't have fires there, it's just a treatment area. You build fires by the river, at the foot of the mountain. I walked on coals, it was so exciting, Natasha! Of course, I got badly burned . . . You need feet with calluses on them, so you don't get burned. You know, it's like those silicon gloves you use to take pans out of the oven. People with lots of calluses on their feet can walk on coals all day without feeling anything. I have calluses, too, but for some reason they didn't help. My feet really hurt that time. Maybe if I do it again, my feet will have some sort of immunity to fire."

"Here's a picture of Stepan sitting with some girl, look, she's so beautiful! How could he not be in love with her? Look at her cute little nose! I don't know, she's just gorgeous. An actress? Yes, an actress . . . remember, you used to want to be an actress, too? But with your looks . . . Of course, a director has power. It's good to be the boss. Though that'll never help you keep a good-looking man. You know what my mom told me: a good-looking man is never yours alone. Understand? Be careful! But really, this girl, she's incredible. Very beautiful."

"Look, you're obviously very

high-strung. When you were little, you were so sweet, you listened to me. Such a sweetheart! Always hugging me! How come you're so rude now?"

"MOM, I'M GOING FOR A SMOKE AND THEN TO BED."

Mom, I'm going for a smoke and then to bed, and I'm also gonna get drunk. You're saying the most ridiculous bullshit, I can't listen to it unless I'm drunk.

I just can't while sober, I'm sorry. My blood starts to boil. It's not healthy. I also have medical conditions: one's migraines, the other's alcoholism. Your monologues are triggering them both. Mom, please stop talking. Why can't you just appreciate a quiet evening!

Mom.

I'm not willing to make sacrifices anymore.

Although neither are you . . .

"Mom, what if you stayed a few more days? It's been a year . . ."

"What are you talking about? My dogwood's in bloom, I need to water my tomatoes, I've got my garden, my onions . . ."

"Mom, will you come visit this summer?"

"What do you mean, 'summer'? My tomatoes and cucumbers will be ripe, I've got my bees at home, my chickens . . ."

Well, Mom, this summer I've got my shoots, casting, scouting, rehearsals, editing, footage, all that bullshit . . .

So, Mom.

The point is, we don't need each other.

When did it get like this, you making me crazy and me scaring you?

When was that critical moment when a good psychoanalyst would've concluded: these are two separate people now?

You probably think all this started the moment I got on that plane and flew far away from you. The day I crushed your careful plot for me: the youngest daughter, staying by your bedside and bringing you glasses of water. Best-case scenario, we'd die on the same day. Worst-case, I'd survive you by a year, tops. But no matter what, at least I'd be with you until you died.

But!

In fairy tales, younger daughters go looking for the scarlet flower. So did I. I left, up in a puff of smoke. This traitor was as good as gone.

That's not the point, of course. The point is, right now we're sitting here on the couch, two strangers. You're touching my shoulder and I'm trembling in protest.

How, when, why did this happen? This blind, inconceivable, bleeding love, for which I would have killed without batting an eye, turned into hate. As if I've crossed over to the dark side of the moon.

No way you have the courage to admit to yourself that you haven't loved me for a while now. For you that would be blasphemy, breaking a taboo. You're only capable of loving strangers. Your family is just an obligation. And I want so badly—so badly—to judge you, to rub your face in your own lying, your indifference, your selfishness.

Every time we see each other I waste all our time on this stuff. And once you leave, I sob. I'm so lonely. I miss you. I cry myself into a stupor and give myself stomach cramps. And later I have nightmares where I lose you for-ever . . .

"Mom, why don't you stay three more days . . ."

"I can't do that! I have my chickens at home, Leonid's starting a new job, there's no one to feed the chickens, and the seedlings are sprouting already . . ."

Mom.

How's this. What if this were it. What if we never saw each other again. First of all, you've got high blood pressure and a bad heart. You're already seventy-two.

Second, I'm an alcoholic, and bad shit could happen to me, too.

In this web of impending deaths, where exactly do chickens and seedlings fit in, Mom? What sort of pedestal have we put them on?

Where do shoots and editing fit in? Or money problems, or the producers' voices descending on me from the skies?

Why the fuck do we make an effort to meet once a year, so you can spend a week watching me stress over work and

I can have conversations with you about chickens and other stupid shit?

But whatever. Even if we threw the chickens and the producers out the window (they're basically the same—both need tending, at the expense of all human dignity). Imagine we had all the time in the world. What would we do?

I can answer that with almost 100 percent certainty.

I'd get upset at all the sentences that came out of your mouth, because of their unbelievable stupidity.

You'd be offended and then you'd fake, if not fainting, then dizziness, until I felt sorry for you.

It's the same thing every year.

Maybe if we lived together, some sort of catastrophe would've happened already. But as it is . . . we're a mother and daughter living in forced separation.

I shrink from physical contact. You instigate it.

You try to preserve my younger self, the gentle, zit-ridden, energetic girl who sang and danced Indian dances in the rain with you. The girl who cried at the top of her lungs when she found out the cat had eaten a mouse. The girl who hugged you and talked to aliens in her sleep to impress you, to shock you, to get attention, to let you know in this stupid way that she was special, not like everyone else. The girl who wrote scandalous stories with explicit sexual details so you'd notice she was mature.

And later that already-grown girl who guarded you, never letting you make mistakes, always staying close, beating up your men, protecting you, giving liters of blood to save you, always with you. Always on your side, no matter what. Basically, you've always needed

that girl—the one who still doesn't completely understand you.

I, on the other hand, am trying to
pull away from this new, unwelcome,
distorted you. Because that's exactly
how I see you now. Because I've come
to understand. And now, at my mature
age, I can't fucking believe this is how
things turned out.

You try to resurrect the past. All
we had together, that solidarity, that
feeling of us against the world. Against
all my fathers, all our relatives, all our
neighbors, and everyone who gave us
side-eye at the store.

Our songs in the grass. Me and you,
Mom. We sang nonstop, like crickets,
as the sun went down. We loved going
to the field to watch the sunset. I loved
that . . . We walked in the blossoming
apple orchard. You were always singing or coming up with poems. I sang

along and also thought up things about spring and snowdrops. We loved each other fiercely, and I always—listen—I always felt your heart, your warmth.

And now you try to resurrect the past. You're always trying to remember things: what did I care about before my enlightenment? And I . . .

I'm trying to set aside the present.

I'm sorry. I can't call today. I get upset as soon as I do.

It's such a nice evening, my husband's here, I want to spend time on Facebook. I'm not calling. I'll do it tomorrow.

Tomorrow comes. It's a beautiful morning. I need to make breakfast for Sasha, write my screenplay, and then I have a meeting. Friends come over, I get drunk. Then it's evening again, and I still want to keep things peaceful, not painful. But as soon as I call, that's what it's going to be. Because of your help-less voice, because of my idiotic irri-tation. Because I'm not there with you (even though I didn't want to be). Why is everything so painful, anyway? Oh, because I'm not there . . .

You're scared of me and my short temper, so you lie a lot. Lying is your new thing. Even though you're—let me repeat—seventy-two years old, and you've started to lose your memory, so you mix up your own statements. That's why your lying isn't even lying. It's a personality quirk. That's all.

That's why almost all our conversa-tions are pointless. You rip them out of your memory like turning the page of a newspaper.

I remember a scene from this great documentary, where the granddaughter comes to her grandma with important questions, but the grandma isn't totally there anymore. Or she's pretending not to be. She doesn't remember anything, doesn't give a single answer.

That's how you are, never really answering any of my painful questions. And I get it. It's not easy, answering adult children's questions about why things were the way they were during their childhood.

Why, Mom, why did you always go around acting like a friend or a classmate, able to listen and cry with me, but unable to protect me?

I'll never get an answer. Impossible. All you have in response are tears and pursed lips.

And you say:

"Come on, sweetheart, we're all alive and well, come on!"

"Come on, sweetheart, you've always been so independent, I trusted you."

"Come on, sweetheart, remember,

you said you didn't want to go to school anymore, we bought you a certificate, at the market, remember? And our whole family went crazy, they thought you'd become a cleaning lady, but you became a director, see?"

"Come on, sweetheart, remember, when you were thirteen I left you alone at the beach. I trusted your good sense. You've always been more mature than me! It's like you were born that way . . ."

"Come on, why are you screaming again?"

I scream, Mom. I scream at night, too. I'm a screamer. Yes, I'm rude. Sometimes I scream swear words at you, at your tomatoes and your bees. I'll never get an answer. No matter how much I torture you, no matter what revelations I share.

None of this has anything to do with your current life. Or mine. Now I'm

Sasha's mom, and some nights I don't even scream with hatred. And (guess what?) I don't even want an answer that badly anymore. There just isn't one. That's life, we're alive and well, what more do you want. Everything's sinking down—good, let it drown in the dirty Anapka River. You won't even be able to see what's lost.

Don't reopen your wounds, don't talk about, remember, or touch what's scary, don't wake the bear, don't draw your swords. Let's put it aaaaall to bed, Mom, in our vineyard valley where the stars shine so brightly. I'll never forget that valley, Mom. Like that classic paradox about love and blindness.

And when you die (if I'm still alive), I'll scream at myself for having screamed at you.

Whenever I think about you, I tremble, Mom. Your childlike weakness, your helplessness—they're my greatest heartbreak.

I can accept you, I can accept you.

But—I can't. I'm too disappointed.

I often dream about our house, the one I hate, the one that pulls me back like a magnet. Our stuffy, mosquito-y apartment with creaking wooden floors and cockroaches, and that balcony . . . I often dream I'm down below on the street, looking up at our balcony, and I see the light on and I think, as long as the light's on that means you're there, you're alive. But I can't go into the building and walk upstairs. I'm standing there in my dream like an idiot, watching. And in my dream, I wonder whether I even want to go upstairs and see that place again, supposedly my home, but not really mine at all.

And the grass around it is so green, so tall.

You and I used to lie in that grass. I wanted to lie like that forever.

I wished our grass had never seen Uncle Sasha, your sleepwalking indifference, your heart attacks, your yellow cowardice, or my red hatred.

Mom.

Let's lie a little longer in our green, green grass and look at our balcony, where the lights are on, where you are. And let's sing this song together—you in your open-mouthed Kuban style, me in my out-of-tune falsetto:

"We have mountains, we have plains,
We have windiness and wilderness.
We are children of the stars
But more than any other,
We belong to you, we're yours,
The eaaaaaarth is our mooooother."

Thank you all
for your support.
We do this for you,
and could not do
it without you.

DEEP
VELLUM

PARTNERS

pixel ||| texel

EMBREY FAMILY
FOUNDATION

ALLRED
CAPITAL MANAGEMENT
of
RAYMOND JAMES®

<u>ADDITIONAL DONORS</u>, CONT'D

Mark Haber
Mary Cline
Maynard Thomson
Michael Reklis
Mike Soto
Mokhtar Ramadan
Nikki & Dennis Gibson
Patrick Kukucka
Patrick Kutcher
Rev. Elizabeth & Neil Moseley
Richard Meyer

Scott & Katy Nimmons
Sherry Perry
Sydneyann Binion
Stephen Harding
Stephen Williamson
Susan Carp
Susan Ernst
Theater Jones
Tim Perttula
Tony Thomson

<u>SUBSCRIBERS</u>

Joseph Rebella
Michael Lighty
Shelby Vincent
Margaret Terwey
Ben Fountain
Ryan Todd
Gina Rios
Elena Rush
Courtney Sheedy
Caroline West

Ned Russin
Laura Gee
Valerie Boyd
Brian Bell
Charles Dee Mitchell
Cullen Schaar
Harvey Hix
Jeff Lierly
Elizabeth Simpson
Michael Schneiderman

Nicole Yurcaba
Sam Soule
Jennifer Owen
Melanie Nicholls
Alan Glazer
Michael Doss
Matt Bucher
Katarzyna Bartoszynska
Anthony Brown
Elif Ağanoğlu

AVAILABLE NOW FROM DEEP VELLUM

MICHÈLE AUDIN · *One Hundred Twenty-One Days* · translated by Christiana Hills · FRANCE

BAE SUAH · *Recitation* · translated by Deborah Smith · SOUTH KOREA

MARIO BELLATIN · *Mrs. Murakami's Garden* · translated by Heather Cleary · MEXICO

EDUARDO BERTI · *The Imagined Land* · translated by Charlotte Coombe · ARGENTINA

CARMEN BOULLOSA · *Texas: The Great Theft* · *Before* · *Heavens on Earth*
translated by Samantha Schnee · Peter Bush · Shelby Vincent · MEXICO

MAGDA CARNECI · *FEM* · translated by Sean Cotter · ROMANIA

LEILA S. CHUDORI · *Home* · translated by John H. McGlynn · INDONESIA

MATHILDE CLARK · *Lone Star* · translated by Martin Aitken · DENMARK

SARAH CLEAVE, ed. · *Banthology: Stories from Banned Nations* ·
IRAN, IRAQ, LIBYA, SOMALIA, SUDAN, SYRIA & YEMEN

LOGEN CURE · *Welcome to Midland: Poems* · USA

ANANDA DEVI · *Eve Out of Her Ruins* · translated by Jeffrey Zuckerman · MAURITIUS

PETER DIMOCK · *Daybook from Sheep Meadow* · USA

CLAUDIA ULLOA DONOSO · *Little Bird,* translated by Lily Meyer · PERU/NORWAY

ROSS FARRAR · *Ross Sings Cheree & the Animated Dark: Poems* · USA

ALISA GANIEVA · *Bride and Groom* · *The Mountain and the Wall*
translated by Carol Apollonio · RUSSIA

FERNANDA GARCIA LAU · *Out of the Cage* · translated by Will Vanderhyden · ARGENTINA

ANNE GARRÉTA · *Sphinx* · *Not One Day* · *In/concrete* · translated by Emma Ramadan · FRANCE

JÓN GNARR · *The Indian* · *The Pirate* · *The Outlaw* · translated by Lytton Smith · ICELAND

GOETHE · *The Golden Goblet: Selected Poems* · *Faust, Part One*
translated by Zsuzsanna Ozsváth and Frederick Turner · GERMANY

NOEMI JAFFE · *What are the Blind Men Dreaming?* · translated by Julia Sanches & Ellen Elias-Bursac · BRAZIL

CLAUDIA SALAZAR JIMÉNEZ · *Blood of the Dawn* · translated by Elizabeth Bryer · PERU

PERGENTINO JOSÉ · *Red Ants* · MEXICO

TAISIA KITAISKAIA · *The Nightgown & Other Poems* · USA

JUNG YOUNG MOON · *Seven Samurai Swept Away in a River* · *Vaseline Buddha*
translated by Yewon Jung · SOUTH KOREA

KIM YIDEUM · *Blood Sisters* · translated by Ji yoon Lee · SOUTH KOREA

JOSEFINE KLOUGART · *Of Darkness* · translated by Martin Aitken · DENMARK

YANICK LAHENS · *Moonbath* · translated by Emily Gogolak · HAITI

FORTHCOMING FROM DEEP VELLUM

SHANE ANDERSON · *After the Oracle* · USA

MARIO BELLATIN · *Beauty Salon* · translated by David Shook · MEXICO

MIRCEA CĂRTĂRESCU · *Solenoid*
translated by Sean Cotter · ROMANIA

LEYLÂ ERBIL · *A Strange Woman*
translated by Nermin Menemencioğlu & Amy Marie Spangler· TURKEY

RADNA FABIAS · *Habitus* · translated by David Colmer · CURAÇAO/NETHERLANDS

SARA GOUDARZI · *The Almond in the Apricot* · USA

GYULA JENEI · *Always Different* · translated by Diana Senechal · HUNGARY

UZMA ASLAM KHAN • *The Miraculous True History of Nomi Ali* • PAKISTAN

SONG LIN · *The Gleaner Song: Selected Poems* · translated by Dong Li · CHINA

TEDI LÓPEZ MILLS · *The Book of Explanations* · translated by Robin Myers · MEXICO

JUNG YOUNG MOON · *Arriving in a Thick Fog*
translated by Mah Eunji and Jeffrey Karvonen · SOUTH KOREA

FISTON MWANZA MUJILA · *The Villain's Dance*, translated by Roland Glasser · *The River in the Belly: Selected Poems*, translated by Bret Maney · DEMOCRATIC REPUBLIC OF CONGO

LUDMILLA PETRUSHEVSKAYA · *Kidnapped: A Crime Story*, translated by Marian Schwartz · *The New Adventures of Helen: Magical Tales*, translated by Jane Bugaeva · RUSSIA

SERGIO PITOL · *The Love Parade* · translated by G. B. Henson · MEXICO

MANON STEFAN ROS · *The Blue Book of Nebo* · WALES

JIM SCHUTZE · *The Accommodation* · USA

SOPHIA TERAZAWA · *Winter Phoenix: Testimonies in Verse* · POLAND

BOB TRAMMELL · *Jack Ruby & the Origins of the Avant-Garde in Dallas & Other Stories* · USA

BENJAMIN VILLEGAS · *ELPASO: A Punk Story* · translated by Jay Noden · MEXICO